LOVE,
THE FIDDLER

LLOYD OSBOURNE

Love, The Fiddler

Lloyd Osbourne

© 1st World Library – Literary Society, 2004
PO Box 2211
Fairfield, IA 52556
www.1stworldlibrary.org
First Edition

LCCN: 2004195339

Softcover ISBN: 1-4218-0170-1
Hardcover ISBN: 1-4218-0070-5
eBook ISBN: 1-4218-0270-8

Purchase *"Love, The Fiddler"*
as a traditional bound book at:
www.1stWorldLibrary.org/purchase.asp?ISBN=1-4218-0170-1

1st World Library Literary Society is a nonprofit
organization dedicated to promoting literacy by:

- Creating a free internet library accessible from any computer worldwide.
- Hosting writing competitions and offering book publishing scholarships.

Love, The Fiddler
contributed by Tim, Ed & Rodney
in support of
1st World Library Literary Society

TO LEWIS VANUXEM

CONTENTS

THE CHIEF ENGINEER

I

Frank Rignold had never been the favoured suitor, not at least so far as anything definite was concerned; but he had always been welcome at the little house on Commonwealth Street, and amongst the neighbours his name and that of Florence Fenacre were coupled as a matter of course and every old lady within a radius of three miles regarded the match as good as settled. It was not Frank's fault that it was not, for he was deeply in love with the widow's daughter and looked forward to such an end to their acquaintance as the very dearest thing fate could give him. But in these affairs it is necessary to carry the lady with you - and the lady, though she had never said "no," had not yet been prevailed upon to say "yes." In fact she preferred to leave the matter as it was, and boldly forestalling a set proposal, had managed to convey to Frank Rignold that it was her wish he should not make one.

"Let us be good friends," she would say, "and as for anything else, Frank, there's plenty of time to consider that by and by. Isn't it enough already that we like each other?"

Frank did not think it was enough, but he was not

without intuition and willing to accept the little offered him and be grateful - rather than risk all, and almost certainly lose all, by too exigent a suit. For Florence Fenacre was the acknowledged beauty of the town, with a dozen eligible men at her feet, and was more courted and sought after than any girl in the place. The place, to give it its name, was Bridgeport, one of those dead-alive little ports on the Atlantic seaboard, with a dozen factories and some decaying wharves and that tranquil air of having had a past.

The widow and her pretty daughter lived in a low-roofed, red-brick house that faced the street and sheltered a long deep shady garden in the rear. Land and house had been bought with whale oil. Their little income, derived from the rent of three barren and stony farms and amounting to not more than sixty dollars a month, represented a capitalisation of whale oil. Even the old grey church whither they went twice of a Sunday, was whale oil too, and had been built in bygone days by the sturdy captains who now lay all around it under slabs of stone. There amongst them was Florence's father and her grandfather and her great-grandfather, together with the Macys and the Coffins and the Cabotts with whom they had sailed and quarrelled and loved and intermarried in the years now gone. The wide world had not been too wide for them to sail it round and reap the harvests of far-off seas; but in death they lay side by side, their voyages done, their bones mingling in the New England earth.

Frank Rignold too was a son of Bridgeport, and the sea which ran in that blood for generations bade him in manhood to rise and follow it. He had gone into the engine-room, and at thirty was the chief engineer of a cargo boat running to South American ports. He was a

Lloyd Osbourne

fine-looking man with earnest grey eyes; a reader, a student, an observer; self-taught in Spanish, Latin, and French; a grave, quiet gentlemanly man, whose rare smile seemed to light his whole face, and who in his voyages South had caught something of Spanish grace and courtliness. He returned as regularly to Bridgeport as his ship did to New York; and when he stepped off the train his eager steps took him first to the Fenacres' house, his hands never empty of some little present for his sweetheart.

On the occasion of our story his step was more buoyant than ever and his heart beat high with hope, for she had cried the last time he went away, and though no word of love had yet been spoken between them, he was conscious of her increasing inclination for him and her increasing dependence. Having already won so much it seemed as though his passionate devotion could not fail to turn the scale and bring her to that admission he felt it was on her lips to make. So he strode through the narrow streets, telling himself a fairy story of how it all might be, with a little house of their own and she waiting for him on the wharf when his ship made fast; a story that never grew stale in the repetition, but which, please God, would come true in the end, with Florence his wife, and all his doubtings and heart-aches over.

Florence opened the door for him herself and gave a little cry of surprise and welcome as they shook hands, for in all their acquaintance there had never been a kiss between them. It was all he could do not to catch her in his arms, for as she smiled up at him, so radiant and beautiful and happy, it seemed as if it were his right and that he had been a fool to have ever questioned her love for him. He followed her into the sitting-room, laughing like a child with pleasure and thrilled through and through with the sound of her voice and the touch of her hand and the vague, subtle perfume of her whole being. His laughter died away, however, as he saw what the room contained. Over the chairs, over the sofa, over the table, in the stacked and open pasteboard boxes on the floor, were dresses and evening gowns outspread with the profusion of a splendid shop, and even to his unpractised eyes, costly and magnificent beyond anything he had ever seen before. Florence swept an opera cloak from a chair and made him sit down, watching him the while with a charming gaiety and excitement. At such a moment it seemed to him positively heartless.

"Florence," he said, almost with a gasp, "does this mean that you are going to be -" He stopped short. He could not say that word.

"I'm never going to marry anybody," she returned.

"But -" he began again.

"Then you haven't heard!" she cried, clasping her hands. "Oh, Frank, you haven't heard!"

"I have only just got back," he said.

"I've been left heaps of money," she exclaimed, "from my uncle, you know, the one that treated father so badly and tricked him out of the old manor farm. I hardly knew he existed till he died. And it's not only a lot, Frank, but it's millions!"

He repeated the word with a kind of groan.

"They are probating the will for six," she went on, not noticing his agitation, "but I'm sure the lawyers are making it as low as they can for the taxes. And it's the most splendid kind of property - rows of houses in the heart of New York and big Broadway shops and skyscrapers! Frank, do you realise I own two office buildings twenty stories high?"

Frank tried to congratulate her on her wonderful good fortune, but it was like a voice from the grave and he could not affect to be glad at the death-knell of all his hopes.

"That lets me out," he said.

"My poor Frank, you never were in," she said, regarding him with great kindness and compassion. "I know you are disappointed, but you are too much a man to be unjust to me."

"Oh, I haven't the right to say a word!" he exclaimed quickly. "On your side it was friends and nothing more. I always understood that, Florence."

He was shocked at her almost imperceptible sigh of relief.

"Of course, this changes everything," she said.

"Yet it would have come if it hadn't been for this," he said. "You were getting to like me better and better. You cried when I last went away. Yes, it would have come, Florence," he repeated, looking at her wistfully.

"I suppose it would, Frank," she said.

"Oh, Florence!" he exclaimed, and could not go on lest his voice should betray him.

"And we should have lived in a poky little house," she said, "and you would have been to sea three-quarters of the time, leaving me to eat my heart out as mother did for father - and it would have been a horrible, dreadful, irrevocable mistake."

"I didn't have to go to sea," he said, snatching at this crumb of hope. "There are other jobs than ships. Why, only last trip I was offered a refrigerating plant in Chicago!"

He did not tell her it bore a salary of four hundred dollars a month and that he had meant to lay it at her feet that morning. In the light of her millions that sum, so considerable an hour before, had suddenly shrunk to nothing. How puny and pitiful it seemed in the contrast. He had a sense that everything had shrunk to nothing - his life, his hopes, his future.

"I know you think I am cruel," she said, in the same calm, considerate tone she had used throughout. "But I never gave you any encouragement, Frank - not in the way you wanted or expected. You were the only person I knew who was the least bit cultivated and nice and travelled and out of the commonplace. I can't tell you how much you brightened my life here, or how glad I was when you came or how sorry I was when you went away - but it wasn't love, Frank - not the love you wished for or the love I feel I have the power to give."

"Why did you let me go on then?" he broke out, "I getting deeper and deeper into it and you knowing all the time it never could come to anything? Just because no words were said, did that make you blind? If you were such a friend of mine as you said you were, wouldn't it have been kinder to have shown me the door and tell me straight out it was hopeless and impossible? Oh, Florence, you took my love when you wanted it, like a person getting warm at a fire, and now when you don't need it any longer you tell me quite unconcernedly that it is all over between us!"

"It would sound so heartless to tell you the real truth, Frank," she said.

"Oh, let me hear it!" he said. "I'm desperate enough for anything - even for that, I suppose."

"I knew it would end the way you wanted it, Frank," she said. "You were getting to mean more and more to me. I did not love you exactly and I did not worry a particle when you were away, but I sort of acquiesced in what seemed to be the inevitable. I know I am horribly to blame, but I took it for granted we'd drift on and on - and this time, if you had asked me, I had made up my mind to say 'yes.'"

She said this last word in almost a whisper, frightened at the sight of Frank's pale face. She ran over to him, and throwing her arms around his neck kissed him again and again.

"We'll always be friends, Frank," she said. "Always, always!"

He made no movement to return her caresses. Her kisses humiliated him to the quick. He pushed her away from him, and when he spoke it was with dignity and gentleness.

"I was wrong to reproach you," he said. "I can appreciate what a difference all this money makes to you. It has lifted you into another world - a world where I cannot hope to follow you, but I can be man enough to say that I understand - that I acquiesce - without bitterness."

"I never liked you so well as I do now, Frank," she said.

"We will say nothing more about it," he said. "I couldn't blame you because you don't love me, could I? I ought rather instead to thank you - thank you for so much you have given me these two years past, your friendship, your intimacy, your trust. That it all came to nothing was neither your fault nor mine. It was your uncle's for dying and leaving you sky-scrapers!"

They both laughed at this, and Frank, now apparently quite himself again, brought forth his presents: a large box of candy, a beautifully bound little volume of Pierre Loti, and a lace collar he had picked up at Buenos Ayres. This last seemed a trifling piece of finery in the midst of all those dresses, though he had paid sixteen dollars for it and had counted it cheap at the price. Florence received it with exaggerated gratitude, genuine enough in one way, for she was touched; but, in spite of herself, her altered fortunes and the memory of those great New York shops, where she had ordered right and left, made the bit of lace seem common and scarce worth possessing. Even as she thanked him she was mentally presenting it to one of the poor Miss Browns who sang in the church choir.

They spent an hour in talking together, eluding on either side any further reference to the subject most in their thoughts and finding safety in books and the little gossip of the place and the news of the day. It might have been an ordinary call, though Frank, as a special favour, was allowed to smoke a cigar, and there was a strained look in Florence's face that gave the lie to her previous professions of indifference. She knew she was violating her own heart, but her character was already corrupting under the breath of wealth, and her head was turned with dreams of social conquests and of a great and splendid match in the roseate future. She kept telling herself how lucky it was that the money had not come too late, and wondering at the same time whether she would ever again meet a man who had such a compelling charm for her as Frank Rignold, and whose mellow voice could move her to the depths. At last, after a decent interval, Frank said he would have to leave, and she accompanied him to the door, where he begged her to remember him to her mother and added something congratulatory about the great good fortune that had befallen her.

"And now good-bye," he said.

"But you will come back, Frank?" she exclaimed anxiously.

"Oh, no!" he said. "I couldn't, Florence, I couldn't."

"I cannot let you go like this," she protested. "Really I can't, Frank. I won't!"

"I don't see very well how you can help it," he said.

"Surely my wish has still some weight with you,"

she said.

"Florence," he returned, holding her hand very tight, "you must not think it pique on my part or anything so petty and unworthy; but I'd rather stop right here than endure the pain of seeing you get more and more indifferent to me. It is bound to come, of course, and it would be less cruel this way than the other."

"You never can have loved me!" she exclaimed. "Didn't I say I wanted to be friends? Didn't I kiss you?"

"Yes," he said slowly, "as you might a child, to comfort him for a broken toy. Florence," he went on, "I have wanted you for the last two years and now I have lost you. I must face up to that. I must meet it with what fortitude I can. But I cannot bear to feel that every time I come you will like me less; that others will crowd me out and take my place; that the gulf will widen and widen until at last it is impassable. I am going while you still love me a little and will miss me. Good-bye!"

She leaned her head on his shoulder and sobbed. She had but to say one word to keep him, and yet she would not say it. Her heart seemed broken in her breast, and yet she let him go, sustained in her resolve by the thought of her great fortune and of the wonderful days to come.

"Good-bye," she said, and stood looking after him as he walked slowly away.

"Oh, that money, I hate it!" she exclaimed to herself as she went in. "I wish he had never left it to me. I didn't want it or expect it or anything, and I should have been happy, oh, so happy!" Then, with a pang, she recalled the refrigerating plant, and the life so quiet and poor and simple and sweet that she and Frank would have led had not her millions come between them.

"Her millions!"

It was inspiriting to repeat those two words to herself. It strengthened her resolve and made her feel how wise she had been to break with Frank. Perhaps, after all, it were better for him not to come back. He was right about the gulf between them, and even since his departure it was widening appreciably.

Then she realised what all rich people realise sooner or later.

"I don't own all that money," she said to herself. "IT OWNS ME!" And with that she went indoors and cried part of the forenoon and spent the rest of it in trying on her new clothes.

Wealth, if it did not bring happiness, at least brought some pleasant distractions.

II

It was fully a year before Frank saw her again; a long year to him, soberly passed in his shipboard duties, with recurring weeks ashore at New York and Buenos Ayres. He had grown more reserved and silent than before; fonder of his books; keener in his taste for abstract science. He avoided his old friends and made no new ones. The world seemed to be passing him while he stood still. He wondered how others could laugh when his own heart was so heavy, and he preferred to go his own way, solitary and unnoticed, taking an increasing pleasure in his isolation. He continued to write to Bridgeport, for there were a few old friends whom he could not disregard altogether, though he made his letters as infrequent as he could and as short. In return he was kept informed of Florence's movements; of the sensation she made everywhere; of the great people who had taken her under their wing; of her rumoured engagements; of her triumphs in Paris and London; of her yachts and horses and splendour and beauty. His correspondents showed an artless pride in the recital. It was becoming their only claim to consideration that they knew Florence Fenacre. Her dazzling life reflected a sort of glory upon themselves, and their letters ran endlessly on the same theme. It was all a modern fairy tale, and they fairly bubbled with satisfaction to think that they knew the fairy princess!

Frank read it all with exasperation. It tormented him to even hear her name; to be reminded of her in any way; to realise that she was as much alive as he himself, and not the phantom he would have preferred to keep her in his memory. Yet he was inconsistent enough to rage when a letter came that brought no news of her. He would tear it into pieces and throw it out of his cabin window. The fools, why couldn't they tell him what he wanted to know! He would carry his ill-humour into the engine-room and revenge himself on fate and the loss of the woman he loved by a harsh criticism of his subordinates. A defective pump or a troublesome valve would set his temper flaming; and then, overcome at his own injustice, he would go to the other extreme; and, roundly blaming himself, would slap some sullen artificer on the back and tell him that it was all a joke. His men, amongst themselves, called him a wild cracked devil, and it was the tattle of the ship that he drank hard in secret. They knew something was wrong with him, and fastened on the likeliest cause. Others said out boldly that the chief engineer was going crazy.

One morning as they were running up the Sound, homeward-bound, they passed a large steam yacht at anchor. Frank happened to be on deck at the time, and he joined with the rest in the little chorus of admiration that went up at the sight of her.

"That's the Minnehaha," said the second mate. "She belongs to the beautiful heiress, Miss Fenacre!"

"Ready for a Mediterranean cruise," said the purser, who had been reading one of the newspapers the pilot had brought aboard.

Frank heard these two remarks in silence. The sun, to him, seemed to stop shining. The morning that had been so bright and pleasant all at once overcame him with disgust. The might-have-been took him by the throat. He descended into the engine-room to hide his dejected face in the heated oily atmosphere below; and seating himself on a tool-chest he watched, with hardly seeing eyes, the ponderous movement of his machinery.

It was the anodyne for his troubles, to feel the vibration of the engines and hear the rumble and hiss of the jacketed cylinders. It always comforted him; he found companionship in the mighty thing he controlled; he looked at the trembling needle in the gauge, and instinctively noted the pressure as he thought of the trim smart vessel at anchor and of his dear one on the eve of parting. He wondered whether they would ever pass again, he and she, in all the years to come.

The thought of the yacht haunted him all that day. He took a sudden revulsion against the grinding routine of his own life. It came over him like a new discovery, that he was tired of South America, tired of his ship, tired of everything. He contrasted his own voyages in and out, from the same place to the same place, up and down, up and down, as regular as the swing of a pendulum with that gay wanderer of the raking masts who was free to roam the world. It came over him with an insistence that he, too, would like to roam the world, and see strange places and old marble palaces with steps descending into the blue sea water, and islands with precipices and beaches and palm trees.

Almost awed at his own presumption he sat down and wrote to Miss Fenacre.

It was a short note, formally addressed, begging her for a position in the engine-room staff. He knew, he said, that the quota was probably made up, and that he could not hope for an important place. But if she would take him as a first-class artificer he would be more than grateful, and ventured on the little pleasantry that even if he had to be squeezed in as a supernumerary he was confident he could save her his pay and keep a good many times over.

He got an answer a couple of days later, addressed from a fashionable New York hotel and granting him an interview. She called him "dear Frank," and signed herself "ever yours," and said that of course she would give him anything he wanted, only that she would prefer to talk it over first.

He put on his best clothes and went to see her, being shown into a large suite on the second floor, where he had to wait an hour in a lofty anteroom with no other company but a statue of Pocahontas. He was oppressed by the gorgeousness of the surroundings - by the frowning pictures, the gilt furniture, the onyx-topped tables, the vases, the mirrors, the ornate clocks. He was in a fever of expectation, and could not fight down his growing timidity. He had not seen Florence for a year, and his heart would have been as much in his mouth had the meeting been set in the old brick house at Bridgeport. At least he said so to himself, not caring to confess that he was daunted by the magnificence of the apartment.

At length the door opened and she came in. She stood for a moment with her hand on the knob and looked at him; then she came over to him with a little rush and took his outstretched hand. He had forgotten how beautiful she was, or probably he had never really known, as he had never beheld her before in one of those wonderful French creations that cost each one a fortune. He stumbled over his words of greeting, and his hand trembled as he held hers.

"Oh, Frank," she said, noticing his agitation. "Are you still silly enough to care?"

"I am afraid I do, Florence," he said, blushing like a boy at her unexpected question. "What's the good of asking me that?"

"You are looking handsome, Frank," she ran on. "I am proud of you. You have the nicest hair of any man I know!"

"I daren't say how stunning you look, Florence," he returned.

"Frank," she said, slowly, fixing her lustrous eyes on his face, "you usen't to be so grave. ... I don't think you have smiled much lately ... you are changed."

He bore her scrutiny with silence.

"Poor boy!" she exclaimed, impulsively taking his hand. "I'm the most heartless creature in the whole world. Do you know, Frank, though I look so nice and girlish, I am really a brute; and when I die I am sure to go to hell."

"I hope not," he said, smiling.

"Oh, but I know!" she cried. "All I ever do is to make people miserable."

"Perhaps it's the people's fault, for - for loving you, Florence," he said.

"It's awfully exciting to see you again," she went on. "You came within an ace of being my husband. I might have belonged to you and counted your washing. It's queer, isn't it? Thrilling!"

"Why do you bring all that up, Florence?" he said. "It's done. It's over. I - I would rather not speak of it."

"But it was such an awfully near thing, Frank," she persisted. "I had made up my mind to take you, you know. I had even looked over my poor little clothes and had drawn a hundred dollars out of the savings bank!"

"You don't take much account of a hundred dollars now," he returned, trying to smile.

"I know you don't want to talk about it," she said, "but I do. I love to play with emotions. I suppose it's a habit, like any other," she continued, "and it grows on one like opium or morphine. That's why I'll go to hell, Frank. It wasn't that way at all when you used to know me. I think I must have been nice then, and really worth loving!"

"Oh, yes!" he returned miserably. "Oh, yes!"

"I have a whole series of the most complicated emotions about you," she said, "only a lot of them are unexploded, like fire crackers before they are touched off. If I lost all my money I'd be in a panic till you came and took me; but as long as I have it I don't think of you more than once a week. Yet, do you know, Frank, if you got a sweetheart, I believe I'd scratch her eyes out. It's rather fine of me to tell you all that," she went on, with a smile, "for I'm giving you the key of the combination, and you might take advantage of it!"

"Florence," he said, "I thought at first you were just laughing at me, but I see that you are right. You are heartless. You oughtn't to talk like that."

She looked a shade put out.

"Well, Frank, it's the truth, anyway," she said, "and in the old days we were always such sticklers for the truth - for sincerity, you know - weren't we?"

"I have no business to correct you," he said humbly. "I resigned all my pretensions that morning in the old house."

"Well, so long as you love me still!" she exclaimed, with a little mocking laugh. "That's the great thing, isn't it? I mean for me, of course. I am greedy for love. It makes me feel so safe and comfortable to think there are whole rows of men that love me. When you have a great fortune you begin to appreciate the things that money cannot buy."

"Oh, your money!" he said. That word in her mouth always stung him.

"Well, you ought to hate my money," she remarked cheerfully. "It queered you, didn't it? And then all rich people are detestable, anyway - selfish to the core, and horrid. Do you know that sometimes when I have flirted awfully with a man at a dinner or somewhere, and the next day he telephones - and the telephone is in the next room - I've just said: 'Oh, bother! tell him I'm out,' rather than take the trouble to get up from my chair. And a nice man, too!"

"I thought I might be treated the same way," he said.

"Then you thought wrong, Frank," she returned, with a sudden change from her tone of flippancy and lightness. "I haven't sunk quite as low as that, you know. I meant other people - I didn't mean you, Frank, dear."

This was said with such a little ring of kindness that Frank was moved.

"Then the old days still count for something?" he said.

"Oh, yes!" she said.

"But not enough to hurt?" he ventured.

"Sometimes they do and sometimes they don't," she returned. "It depends on how good a time I'm having. But I hate to think I'm weak and selfish and vain, and that the only person I really care for is myself. I value my self-esteem, and it often gets an awful jar. Sometimes I feel like a girl that has run away from home - diamonds and dyed hair, you know - and then wakes up at night and cries to think of what a price she has paid for all her fine things!" Florence waved her hand towards the alabaster statue of Pocahontas, with a little ripple of self-disdain. She was in a strange humour, and beneath the surface of her apparent gaiety there ran an undercurrent of bitterness and contempt for herself. Her eyes were unusually brilliant, and her cheeks were pink enough to have been rouged. The sight of her old lover had stirred many memories in her bosom.

"And what about my job, Florence?" he said, changing

the conversation. "I've caught the yachting idea, too. Can it be managed?"

"Oh, I want to talk to you about that," she said.

"Well, go on," he said, as she hesitated.

"I am so afraid of hurting your feelings, Frank," she said with a singular timidity.

"My feelings are probably tougher than you think," he returned.

"You will think so badly of me," she said. "You will be affronted."

"It sounds as though you wanted to engage me for your butler," he said. Then, as she still withheld the words on her lips, he went on: "Don't be uneasy about saying it, Florence. If it's impossible - why, that's the end of it, of course, and no harm done."

"I want you to come," she said simply.

"Then, what's the trouble?" he demanded, getting more and more mystified. "I don't mind being an artificer the least bit. I like to work with my hands. I'm a good mechanic, and I like it."

"I want you for my chief engineer," she said.

This was news, indeed. Frank's face betrayed his keen pleasure. He had never soared to the heights of asking or expecting THAT.

"I had to dismiss the last one," she went on. "That's the

reason why I'm still here, and not two days out, as I had expected. He locked himself in his cabin and shot at people through the door, and told awful lies to the newspapers."

"If it's anything about my qualifications," he said, thinking he had found the reason of her backwardness, "I don't fancy I'll have any trouble to satisfy you. I don't want to toot my own horn, Florence, but really, you know, I am rated a first-class man. I'll prove that by my certificates and all that, or give me two weeks' trial, and see for yourself."

"Oh, it isn't that," she said.

"Then, what is it?" he broke out. "Only the other day they offered me a Western Ocean liner, and, if you like, I'll send you the letter. If I am good enough for a big passenger ship, I guess I can run the Minnehaha to please you!"

"Frank," she returned, "it is not a question of your competency at all. You know very well I'd trust my life to you, blindfold. It's - it's the social side, the old affair between us, the first names and all that kind of thing."

"Oh, I see!" he said blankly.

"As an officer on my ship," she said, "you could easily put yourself and me in a difficult position. In a way, we'll really be further apart than if you were in South America and I in Monte Carlo, for, though we'd always be good friends, and all that, the formalities would have to be observed. Now, I have offended you?" she added, putting out her hand appealingly.

"I think you might have known me better, Florence," he returned. "I am not offended - what right have I to be offended - only a little hurt, perhaps, to think that you could doubt me for a single moment in such a matter. I understand very well, and appreciate the need for it. Did you expect me to call you Florence on the quarterdeck of your own vessel, and presume on our old friendship to embarrass you and set people talking? Good Heavens, what do you take me for?"

"Don't be angry with me, Frank," she pleaded. "It had to be said, you know. I wanted you so much to come; I wanted to share my beautiful vessel with you; and yet I dreaded any kind of a false position."

"I shall treat you precisely as I would any owner of any ship I sailed on," he said. "That is, with respect and always preserving my distance. I will never address you first except to say good-morning and good-evening, and will show no concern if you do not speak to me for days on end."

"Oh, Frank, you are an angel!" she cried.

"No," he returned, "only - as far as I can - a gentleman, Miss Fenacre."

"We needn't begin now, Frank," she exclaimed, almost with annoyance.

"Am I in your service?" he asked.

"From to-day," she answered, "and I will give you a note to Captain Landry."

"Then you will be Miss Fenacre to me from now on,"

he said.

"You must say good-bye to Florence first," she said, smiling. "You may kiss my hand," she said, as she gave it to him. "You used to do it so gallantly in the old days - such a Spaniard that you are, Frank - and I liked it so much!"

He did so, and for the first time in his life with a kind of shame.

"I hope we are not both of us making a terrible mistake, Florence," he said.

"Oh, I couldn't want a better chief!" she said, "and, as for you, it's the wisest thing you ever did. It's me, after all, who is making the sacrifice, for, in a month or two, all the gilt will wear off, and you will see me as I really am. You will find it very disillusioning to go to sea with your divinity," she added. "You will discover she is a very flesh-and-blood affair, after all, Frank, and not worth the tip of your little finger."

"I had a good many opportunities of judging before," he replied, "and the more I knew her the more I loved her."

"Well, I am changed now," she said. "I suppose all the bad has come to the surface since - like the slag when they melt iron and skim it off with dippers - only with me there's nobody to dip. If *I* am astounded at the difference, what do you suppose you'll be?"

"There never could be any difference to me," he said.

"That's the only kind of love worth talking about," she

said, going to the window and looking out.

For a while neither of them spoke. Frank rose and stood with his hat in his hand, waiting to take his departure. Florence turned, and going to an escritoire sat down and wrote a few lines on a card.

"Present this to Captain Landry," she said, "and, now, my dear chief engineer, I will give you your conge."

He thanked her, and put the card carefully in his pocketbook.

"What a farce it all is, Frank!" she broke out. "There's something wrong in a system that gives a girl millions of dollars to do just as she likes with. I don't care what they say to the contrary; I believe women were meant to belong to men, to live in semi-slavery and do what they are told, to bring up children and travel with the pots and pans, and find their only reward in pleasing their husbands."

"I wouldn't care to pass an opinion," said Frank. "Some of them are happy that way, no doubt."

"What does anybody want except to be happy?" she continued, in the same strain of resentment. "Isn't that what all are trying for as hard as they can? I'd like to go out in the street and stop people as they came along and ask them, the one after the other: 'Would you tell me if you are happy?' And the one that said 'yes' I'd give a hundred dollars to!"

"As like as not it would be some shabby fellow with no overcoat," said Frank.

"Now you can go away!" she exclaimed suddenly. "I don't know what's the matter with me, Frank. I think I'm going to cry! Go, go!" she cried imperiously, as he still stood there.

Frank bowed and obeyed, and his last glimpse, as he closed the door, was of her at the window, looking down disconsolately into the street below.

III

Spring was well begun when the Minnehaha sailed for Europe to take her place in the mimic fleets that were already assembling. As like seeks like, so the long, swift white steamer headed like a bird for her faraway companions, and arrived amongst them with colours flying, and her guns roaring out salutes. By herself she was greedy for every pound of steam and raced her engines as though speed were a matter of life and death; but, once in company, she was content to lag with the slowest, and suit her own pace to the stately progress of the schooners and cutters that moved by the wind alone. She found friends amongst all nations, and, in that cosmopolitan society of ships, dipped her flag to those of England, France, Holland, Belgium, and Germany.

It was a wonderful life of freedom and gaiety. A great yacht carries her own letter of introduction, and is accorded everywhere the courtesies of a man-of-war, to whom, in a sense, she is a sister. Official visits are paid and returned; naval punctilio reigns; invitations are lavished from every side. There is, besides, a free-masonry amongst those splendid wanderers of the sea, a transcendent Bohemianism, that puts them nearly all upon a common footing. A holiday spirit is in the air, and kings and princes who at home are hidden within walls of triple brass, here unbend like children out of school, and make friends and gossip about their neighbours and show off their engine-rooms and their ice plant and some new idea in patent boat davits after the manner of very ordinary mortals. Not of course that kings and princes predominate, but the same spirit prevailed with those who on shore held their heads very high and practised a jealous exclusiveness. Amongst them all Florence Fenacre was a favourite of favourites. Young, beautiful, and the mistress of a noble fortune, there was everything to cast a glamour about this charming American who had come out of the unknown to take all hearts by storm.

Her haziness about distinctions of rank filled these Europeans with an amused amazement. There was to them something quite royal in her naivety and lack of awe; in her high spirit, her vivacity, and her absolute disregard of those who failed to please her. She convulsed one personage by describing another as "that tiresome old man who's really too disreputable to have tagging around me any longer"; and had a quarrel and a making up with a reigning duke about a lighter of coal that their respective crews had come to blows over. Everybody adored her, and she seldom put to sea without a love-sick yacht in her wake.

Of course, here as elsewhere, every phase of human character was displayed, and most conspicuous of all amongst the evil was the determination of many to win Florence's millions for themselves. Amid that noble concourse of vessels, every one of which stood for a princely income, there were adventurers as needy and as hungry as any sharper in the streets of New York. There is an aristocratic poverty, none the less real because three noughts must be added to all the figures, that first surprised and then disgusted the pretty American. Her first awakening to the fact was when, as a special favour, she sold her best steam launch to a French marquise at the price it had cost her. Though that lady was very profuse with little pink notes and could purr over Florence by the hour, her signature on a cheque was never forthcoming, and our heroine had a fit of fury to think of having been so deceived.

"It was a downright confidence trick," she burst out to the comte de Souvary, firing up afresh with the memory of her wrongs. "I loved my launch. It was a beauty. It never went dotty at the time you needed it most and it was a vertical inverted triple-expansion direct-acting propeller!' (Florence could always rattle off technical details and showed her Americanism in her catalogue-like fluency in this respect.) "And I miss it and I want it back, and the horrid old woman never means to pay me a penny!"

"Oh, my child!" said the count, "she never pays anybody ze penny. She is a stone from which one looks in vain for blood. Your launch is - what do you call it in ze Far Vest - a goner!"

"But she's descended from Charlemagne," cried Florence. "She has the entree to all the courts. She ought to be exposed for stealing my boat!"

"What does anybody do when he is robbed?" said the count philosophically. He could afford to be philosophical: it wasn't HIS vertical inverted triple-expansion direct-acting propeller. "Smile and be more careful ze next time," he went on. "The marquise's reputation is international for what is charitably called her eccentricity."

"In America they put people in jail for that kind of eccentricity!" exclaimed Florence.
"Oh, the best way in Europe is money-with-order," said the count, "what I remember once a friend seeing in that great country of which you are ze ornament - in

God we trust: all others cash!"

"Well, it's a shame," said Florence, "and if I ever get the chance of a dark night I'll ram her with the Minnehaha!"

Florence's mother, a dear little old lady who did tatting and read the Christian Herald, was always the particular target of the fortune-hunters who pursued her daughter. It seemed such a brilliant idea to capture the mother first as the preparatory step of getting into the good graces of the heiress; and the old lady, who was one of the most guileless of her sex, never failed to fall into the trap and take the attentions all in earnest. Comte de Souvary used to say that if you wished to find the wickedest men in Europe you had only to cast your eyes in the direction of Florence's mother; and she would be trotted off to church and driven in automobiles and lunched in casinos by the most notorious and unprincipled scapegraces of the Old World.

Florence, who, like all heiresses, had developed a positive instinct for the men who meant her mischief, was always delighted at the repeated captures of the old lady; and it was an endless entertainment to her when her mother was induced to champion the cause of some aristocratic ne'er-do-well.

"But, Mamma," she would say, "I hate to call your friends names, but really he's a perfect scamp, and underneath all his fine manners he is no better than a wolf ravening for rich young lambs!"

"Oh, Florence, how can you be so uncharitable!" her mother would retort. "If you could only hear the way he speaks of his mother and his ruined life, and how he is trying to be a better man for your sake - "

"Always the same old story," said Florence. "It's wonderful the good I do just sailing around and radiating moral influence. The count says I ought to get a medal from the government with my profile on one side and a composite picture of my admirers on the other! And if I do, Mamsey, I'll give it to you to keep!"

Frank Rignold was sometimes tempted to curse the day that had ever brought him aboard the Minnehaha. To be a silent spectator of gaieties and festivities he could not share; to be condemned to stand aloof while he saw the woman he loved petted and sought after by men of exalted position - what could be imagined more detestable to a lover without hope, without the shadow of a claim, with nothing to look forward to except the inevitable day when a luckier fellow would carry her off before his eyes. He moped in secret and often spent hours locked in his cabin, sitting with his face in his hands, a prey to the bitterest melancholy and dejection. In public, however, he always bore himself unflinchingly, and was too proud a man and too innately a gentleman to allow his face to be read even by her. It was incumbent on him, so long as he drew her pay and wore her uniform, to act in all respects the part he was cast to play; and no one could have guessed, except perhaps the girl herself, that he had any other thought save to do his duty cheerfully and well.

Captain Landry sat in the saloon at the bottom of the table, Florence herself taking the head; but the other officers of the ship had a cosey messroom of their own, presided over by Frank Rignold as the officer second in rank on board. Thus whole days might pass with no further exchange between himself and Florence than the customary good-morning when they happened to meet on deck. Except on the business of the ship it was tacitly understood that no officer should speak to her without being first addressed. The discipline of a man-of-war prevailed; everything went forward with stereotyped precision and formality; the officers were supposed to comport themselves with impassivity and self-effacement. Florence had no more need of being conscious of their presence than if they had been so many automatons.

Her life and theirs offered a strange contrast. She in her little court of idlers and merry-makers; they, the grave men who were answerable for her safety, the exponents of a rigid routine, to whom the clang of the bells brought recurring duties and the exercise of their professional knowledge. To her, yachting was a play: to them, a business.

"I often remark your chief engineer," said the comte de Souvary to Florence. "A handsome man, with an air at once sad and noble - one of zoze extraordinary Americans who keep for their machines the ardour we Europeans lavish on the women we love - and whose spirits when zey die turn without doubt into petrole or electricity."

"I have known Mr. Rignold ever since I was a child," said Florence, pleased to hear Frank praised. "I regard him as one of my best and dearest friends."

"The more to his credit," said the count, astonished. "Many in such a galere would prove themselves presumptuous and troublesome."

"He is almost too much the other way," said Florence, with a sigh.

"Ah, that appeals to me!" said the count. "I should be such anozzer in his place. Proud, silent, unobtrusive, who gives dignity to what otherwise would be a false position."

"I came very near being his wife once," said Florence, impelled, she hardly knew why, to make the confession.

The count was thunderstruck.

"His wife!" he exclaimed.

"Before I was rich, you know," explained Florence. "A million years ago it seems now, when I lived in a little town and was a nobody."

"Anozzer romance of the Far Vest!" cried the count, to whom this term embraced the entire continent from Maine to San Francisco.

Florence was curiously capricious in her treatment of Frank Rignold. Often she would neglect him for weeks together, and then, in a sort of revulsion, would go almost to the other extreme. Sometimes at night, when he would be pacing the deck, she would come and take his arm and call him Frank under her breath and ask him if he still loved her; and in a manner half tender, half mocking, would play on his feelings with a deliberate enjoyment of the pain she inflicted. Her greatest power of torment was her frankness. She would talk over her proposals; weigh one against the other; revel in her self-analysis and solemnly ask Frank his opinion on this or that part of her character. She talked with equal freedom of her regard for himself, and was almost brutal in confessing how hard it was to hold herself back.

"I think I must be awfully wicked, Frank," she said to him once. "I love you so dearly, and yet I wouldn't marry you for anything!" And then she ran on as to whether she ought to take Souvary and live in Paris or Lord Comyngs and choose London. "It's so hard to decide," she said, "and it's so important, because one couldn't change one's mind afterwards."

"Not very well," said Frank.

"You mustn't grind your teeth so loud," she said. "It's compromising."

"I wish you would talk about something else or go away," he said, goaded out of his usual politeness.

"Oh, I love my little stolen tete-a-tetes with you!" she exclaimed. "All those other men are used up, emotionally speaking. The count would turn a neat phrase even if he were to blow his brains out the next minute. They think they are splendidly cool, but it only means that they have exhausted all their powers of sensation. You are delightfully primitive and unspoiled, and then I suppose it is natural to like a fellow-countryman best, isn't it? Now, honest - have you found any girls over here you like as well as me?"

"I haven't tried to find any," said Frank.

"You aren't a bit disillusioned, are you?" she said. "You simply shut your eyes and go it blind. A woman likes that in a man. It's what love ought to be. It's silly of me to throw it away."

"Perhaps it is, Florence," he said. "Who knows but what some day you may regret it?"

"I often think of that," she returned. "I am afraid all the good part of me loves you, and all the bad loves the counts and dukes and earls, you know. And the good is almost drowned in all the rest, like vegetables in vegetable soup."

She excelled in giving such little dampers to sentiment, and laughed heartily at Frank's discomfiture.

"You can be awfully cruel," he said. "I wonder you can be so beautiful when you can think such things and say them. You treat hearts like toys and laugh when you break them."

"Well, there's one thing, Frank," she said seriously. "I have never pretended to you or tried to appear better than I am; and you are the only man I can say that to and not lie!"

IV

The comte de Souvary, towards whom Florence betrayed an inclination that seemed at times to deserve a warmer word, was a French gentleman nearing forty. He was a man of distinguished appearance, with all the gaiety, grace, and charm that, in spite our popular impression to the contrary, are not seldom found amongst the nobles of his country. His undoubted wealth and position redeemed his suit from any appearance of being inspired by a mercenary motive. Indeed, he was accustomed himself to be pursued, and Florence and he recognised in each other a fellowship of persecution.

"We are ze Pale Faces," he would say, "and ze ozzers zey are Indians closing in from every corner of ze Far Vest for our scalps!"

He was, in many ways, the most accomplished man that Florence had ever known. He was a violinist, a singer, a poet, and yet these were but a part of his various gifts; for in everything out of doors he was no less a master and took the first place as though by right. He was the embodiment of everything daring and manly; it seemed natural for him to excel; he simply did not know what fear was. He was always ready to smile and turn a little joke, whether speeding in his automobile at a breakneck pace or ballooning above the clouds in search of what was to him the breath of life: "ze sensation." He could never see a new form of "ze sensation" without running for it like a child for a new toy. His whole attitude towards the world was that of a furious curiosity. He could not bear to leave it, he said, until all he had learned how all the wheels went round. He had stood on the Matterhorn. He had driven the Sud express. He had exhausted lions and tigers. In moods of depression he would threaten to follow Andree to the pole and figure out his plans on the back of an envelope.

"Magnificent!" he would cry, growing instantly cheerful at the prospect. "Think of ze sensation!"

He spoke English fluently, though shaky on the TH and the W, and it was first hand and not mentally translated. His pronunciation of Far West, two words that were constantly on his lips, was an endless entertainment to Florence, and out of a sense of humour she forebore to correct him. It was typical, indeed, of his ignorance of everything American. Europe was at his fingers' ends; there was not a country in it he was not familiar with; intimately familiar, knowing much of what went on behind the scenes, and the lives and characters of the men, and not less the women, who shaped national policies and held the steering-wheels of state.

"Muravief would never do that," he would say. "He is constitutionally inert, and his imagination has carried him through too many unfought wars for him to throw down the gage now. He smokes cigarettes and dreams of endless peace. I had many talks with him last year and found him impatient of any subject but the redemption of the paper rouble!"

But his mind had never crossed the Atlantic Ocean. He still thought that the Civil War had been between North and South America. To him the United States was a vague region peopled with miners, pork-packers, and Indians; a jumble of factories, forests, and red-shirted men digging for gold, all of it fantastically seen through the medium of Buffalo Bill's show. It was a constant wonder to him that such conditions had been able to produce a woman like Florence Fenacre.

"You are the flower of ze prairie," he would say, "an atavism of type, harking back a dozen generations to aristocratic progenitors, having nothing in common with the Pathfinder your Papa!"

"He wasn't a pathfinder," said Florence, "he was a whaler captain."

But this to the count seemed only the more remarkable. He raised the fabric of a fresh romance on the instant, especially (on Florence telling him more about her forebears) when he began to mix up the Pilgrim Fathers, the Revolutionary War, and the Alabama in one brisk panorama of his ever dear "Far Vest"!

Florence's acquaintance with the comte de Souvary went back to Majorca, where, in the course of one of those sudden blows, so common on the Mediterranean, their respective yachts had fled for shelter. His own was a large auxiliary schooner called the Paquita, a lofty, showy vessel which he sailed himself with his usual courage and audacity. He had the reputation of scaring his unhappy guests - when any were bold enough to accept his invitations - to within the prover-bial inch of their lives; and they usually changed "ze sensation" for the nearest mail-boat home. Florence and he had struck up a warm friendship from the start, and for the whole summer their vessels were inseparable, sailing everywhere in company and anch-oring side by side.

The count had a way of courtship peculiarly his own. He made it apparent from the first how deeply he had been stirred by Florence's beauty and how ready he was to offer her his hand; but as a matter of fact he never did so in set terms, and treated her more as a comrade than a divinity. He talked of his own devotion to her as something detached and impersonal, willing as much as she to laugh over it and treat it lightly. He was never jealous, never exacting, and seemed to be as happy to share her with others as when he had her all alone in one of their tete-a-tetes. What he coveted most of all was her intimacy, her confidence, the frank expression of her own true self; and in this exchange he was willing to give as much as he received and often more. Sometimes she was piqued at his apparent indifference - at his lack of any stronger feeling for her - seeming to detect in him something of her own insouciance and coldness.

"You really don't care for me a bit," she said once. "I am only another form of 'ze sensation' - like going up in a balloon or riding on the cow-catcher."

"I keep myself well in hand," he returned. "I am not approaching the terrible age of forty without knowing a little at least about women and their ways."

"A little!" she exclaimed ironically. "You know enough to write a book!"

"Zat book has taught me to go very slow," he said. "Were I in my young manhood I'd come zoop, like that, and carry you off in ze Far Vest style. But I can never hope to be that again with any woman; my decreasing hair forbids, if nozing else - but my way is to make myself indispensable - ze old dog, ze old standby, as you Americans say - the good old harbour to which you will come at last when tired of ze storms outside!"

"Your humility is a new trait," said Florence.

"It's none ze less real because it is often hid," said the count. "I watch you very closely, more closely than perhaps you even think. You have all the heartlessness of youth and health and beauty. I would be wrong to put my one little piece of money on the table and lose all; and so I save and save, and play ze only game that offers me the least chance - ze waiting game!"

"I believe that's true," said Florence.

"Were I to act ze distracted lover, you would laugh in my face," he went on earnestly. "Were I to propose and be refused, my pride would not let me - my instinct as gentleman would not let me - go trailing after you with my long face. The idyll would be over. I would go!"

"There are times when I think a heap of you," said Florence encouragingly.

"Oh, I know so well how it would be," he continued. "A week of doubt - of fever; a rain of little notes; and then with your good clear honest Far Vest sense you would say: No, mon cher, it is eempossible!"

"Yes, I suppose I would," said Florence.

"I would rather be your friend all my life," said the count, "than to be merely one of the rejected. I have no ambition to place my name on that already great list. I have never yet asked a woman to marry me, and when I do I care not for the expectation of being refused!"

"You are like all Europeans," said Florence, "you believe in a sure thing."

"My heart is not on my sleeve," he returned, "and I value it too highly to lose it without compensation."

"It is interesting to hear all your views," said Florence. "I am sure I appreciate the compliment highly. It's a new idea, this of the wolf making a confidant of the lamb."

"Oh, my dear!" he broke out, "I am only a poor devil holding back from committing a great stupidity."

"Is that how you describe marrying me?" she said lightly.

"Ze day will come," he said, disregarding her question, "I think it will - I hope it will - when you will say to me: My dear fellow, I am tired of all this fictitious gaiety; of all this rush and bustle and flirtation; of this life of fever and emptiness. I long for peace and do not know where to find it. I am like a piece of music to whom one waits in vain for the return to the keynote. Tell me where to find it or else I die!"

"Rather forward of me to say all that, Count," observed the girl. "But suppose I did - what then?"

The count opened wide his arms.

"I would answer: here!" he said.

V

Thus the bright days passed, amid animating scenes, with memories of sky and cloud and noble headlands and stately, beautiful ships. Like two ocean sweethearts the Minnehaha and the Paquita took their restless way together, side by side in port, inseparable at sea. At night the one lit the other's road with a string of ruby lanterns and kept the pair in company across the dark and silent water. Their respective crews, not behindhand in this splendid camaraderie of ships, fraternised in wine-shops and strolled through the crooked foreign streets arm in arm. Breton and American, red cap and blue, sixty of the one and eighty of the other - they were brothers all and cemented their friendship in blood and gunpowder, in tattooed names, flags and mottoes, after the time-honoured and artless manner of the sea.

In the drama of life it is often the least important actors who are happiest, and the stars themselves are not always to be the most envied. Florence, torn between her ambition and her love, knew what it was to toss all night on her sleepless bed and wet the pillow with her tears. De Souvary, who found himself every day deeper in the toils of his ravishing American, chafed and struggled with unavailing pangs; and as for Frank Rignold, he endured long periods of black depression as he watched from afar the steady progress of his rival's suit; and his moody face grew moodier and exasperation rose within him to the rebellion point.

By September the two yachts were lying in Cowes, and already there was some talk of winter plans and a possible voyage to India. The count was enthusiastic about the project, as he was about anything that could keep him and Florence together, and he had ordered a stack of books and spent hours at a time with the mistress of the Minnehaha reading over Indian Ocean directories and plotting imaginary courses on the chart.

With the prospect of so extended a trip before him, Frank found much to be done in the engine-room, for their suggested cruise would be likely to carry them far out of the beaten track, and he had to be prepared for all contingencies. A marine engine requires to be perpetually tinkered, and an engineer's duty is not only to run it, but to make good the little defects and break-downs that are constantly occurring. Frank was a daily visitor at the local machine-shop, and his business engagements with Mr. Derwent, the proprietor, led insensibly to others of the social kind.

Derwent's house was close by his works, and Frank's trips ashore soon began to take in both. Derwent had a daughter, a black-haired, black-eyed, pink-cheeked girl, named Cassie, one of those vigorous young English beauties that men would call stunning and women bold. She did not wait for any preliminaries, but straightway fell in love with the handsome American engineer that her father brought home. She made her regard so plain that Frank was embarrassed, and was not a bit put off at his reluctance to play the part she assigned to him.

"That's always my luck," she remarked with disarming candour, "a poor silly fool who always likes them that don't like me and spurns them that do!" And then she added, with a laugh, that he ought to be tied up, "for you are a cruel handsome man, Frank, and my heart goes pitapat at the very sight of you!"

She called him Frank at the second visit; and at the third seated herself on the arm of his chair and took his hand and held it.

"Can't you ever forget that girl in Yankee-land?" she said. "She ain't here, is she, and why shouldn't you steal a little harmless fun? There's men who'd give their little finger to win a kiss from me - and you sit there so glum and solemn, who could have a bushel for the asking!"

For all Frank's devotion to Florence he could not but be flattered at being wooed in this headlong fashion. He was only a man after all, and she was the prettiest girl in port. He did not resist when she suddenly put her arms around him and pressed his head against her bosom, calling him her boy and her darling; but remained passive in her embrace, pleased and yet ashamed, and touched to the quick with self-contempt.

"You mustn't," he said, freeing himself. "Cassie, it's wrong - it's dreadful. You mustn't think I love you, because I don't."

"Yes, but I am going to make you," she said with splendid effrontery, looking at herself in the glass and patting her rumpled hair. "See what you have done to me, you bad boy!"

Had she been older or more sophisticated, Frank would have been shocked at this reversal of the sexes. But in her self-avowed and unashamed love for him she was more like a child than a woman; and her good-humour and laughter besides seemed somehow to belittle her words and redeem the affair from any seriousness. Frank tried to stay away, for his conscience pricked him and he did not care to drift into such an unusual and ambiguous relation with Derwent's handsome daughter. But Cassie was always on the watch for him and he could not escape from the machine-works without falling into one of her ambushes. She would carry him off to tea, and he never left without finding himself pledged to return in the evening. In his loneliness, hopelessness, and desolation he found it dangerously sweet to be thus petted and sought after. Cassie made no demands of him and acquiesced with apparent cheerfulness in the implication that he loved another woman. She humbly accepted the little that was left over, and, though she wept many hot tears in secret, outwardly at least she never rebelled or reproached him. She knew that to do either would be to lose him. In fact she made it very easy for him to come, and gave up her girlish treasure of affection without any hope of reward. Frank, by degrees, discovered a wonderful comfort in being with her. It was balm to his wounds and bruises; and, like someone who had long been out in the cold, he warmed himself, so to speak, before that bright fire, and found himself growing drowsy and contented.

It must not be supposed that all this went on unremarked, or that in the gossip of the yacht Frank and Cassie Derwent did not come in for a considerable share of attention. It passed from the officers' mess to the saloon, and Florence bit her lip with anger and jealousy when the joke went round of the chief engineer's "infatuation." In revenge she treated Frank more coldly than ever, and went out of her way to be agreeable to de Souvary, especially when the former was at hand and could be made a spectator of her lover-like glances and a warmth that seemed to transcend the limits of ordinary friendship. She made herself utterly unhappy and Frank as well. The only one of the trio to be pleased was the count.

She made no objection when Frank asked her permission to show the ship to Derwent and his daughter.

"You must be sure and introduce me," she said, with a sparkle of her eyes that Frank was too unpresumptuous to understand. "They say that she is a raving little beauty and that you are the happy man!"

Frank hurriedly disclaimed the honour.

"Oh, no!" he said. "But she is really very sweet and nice, and I think we owe a little attention to her father."

"Oh, her FATHER!" said Florence, sarcastically emphasising the word.

"I hope you don't think there is anything in it," he exclaimed very anxiously. "I suppose there has been some tittle-tattle - I can read it in your face - but there's not a word of truth in it, not a word, I assure you."

"I don't care the one way or other, Frank," she said. "You needn't explain so hard. What does it matter to me, anyway?" and with that she turned away to cordially greet the count as he came aboard.

The two women met in the saloon. Florence at once assumed the great lady, the heiress, the condescending patrician; Cassie flushed and trembled; and in a buzz of commonplaces the stewards served tea while the two women covertly took each other's measure.

Florence grew ashamed of her own behavior, and, unbending a little, tried to put her guests at ease and led Cassie on to talk. Then it came out about the dance that Derwent and his daughter were to give the following night.

"Frank and me have been arranging the cotillon," said Cassie, and then she turned pink to her ears at having called him by his first name before all those people. "I mean Mr. Rignold," she added, amid everyone's laughter and her own desperate confusion. Florence's laughter rang out as gaily as anyone's, and apparently as unaffectedly, and she rallied Cassie with much good humour on her slip.

"So it's Frank already!" she exclaimed. "Oh, Miss Derwent! don't you trust this wicked chief of mine. He is a regular heart-breaker!"

Cassie cried when Frank and she returned home and sat together on the porch.

"She's a proud, haughty minx," she burst out, "and you love her - and as for me I might as well drown myself."

Frank attempted to comfort her.

"Oh, you needn't try to blind me," she said bitterly. "I - I thought it was a girl in America, Frank, a girl like me - just common and poor and perhaps not as nice as I am. And you know she wouldn't wipe her feet on you," she went on viciously - "she so grand with her yachts and her counts and 'Oh, I think I'll run over to Injya for the winter, or maybe it's Cairo or the Nile,' says she! What kind of a chance have you got there, Frank, you in your greasy over-alls and working for her wages?

Won't you break your heart just like I am breaking mine, I that would sell the clothes off my back for you and follow you all over the world!"

Frank protested that she was mistaken; that it wasn't Miss Fenacre at all; that it was absurd to even think of such a thing.

"Oh, Frank, it's bad enough as it is without your lying to me," she said, quite unconvinced. "You've set your eyes too high, and unhappiness is all that you'll ever get from the likes of her. You're a fool in your way and I'm a fool in mine, and maybe when she's married to the count and done for, you'll mind the little girl that's waiting for you in Cowes!" She took his hand and kissed it, telling him with a sob that she would ever remain single for his sake.

"But I don't want you to, Cassie," he said. "You're talking like a baby. What's the good of waiting when I am never coming back?"

"You say that now," she exclaimed, "but my words will come back to you in Injya when you grow tired of her ladyship's coldness and disdain; and I'm silly enough to think you'll find them a comfort to you out there, with nothing to do but to think and think, and be miserable."

VI

The next day he found Cassie in a more cheerful humour and excited about the dance. The house was all upset and she was busy with a dozen of her girl friends in decorating the hall and drawing-room, taking up the carpets, arranging for the supper and the cloakrooms, and immersed generally in the thousand and one tasks that fall on a hostess-to-be. Frank put himself at her orders and spent the better part of the afternoon in running errands and tacking up flags and branches; and after an hilarious tea, in the midst of all the litter and confusion, he went back to the ship somewhat after five o'clock. As he was pulled out in a shore boat he was surprised to pass a couple of coal lighters coming from the Minnehaha, and to see her winches busily hoisting in stores from a large launch alongside. He ran up the ladder, and seeing the captain asked him what was up.

"Sailing orders, Chief," said Captain Landry, enjoying his amazement. "We'll be off the ground in half an hour, eastward bound!" "But I wasn't told anything," cried Frank. "I never got any orders."

"The little lady said you wasn't to be disturbed," said the captain, "and she took it on herself to order your staff to go ahead. I guess you'll find a pretty good head of steam already!"

Frank ran to the side and called back his boat, giving the man five shillings to take a note at once to Cassie. He had no time for more than a few lines, but he could not go to sea without at least one word of farewell.

They were cutting the anchor and were already under steerage way when Cassie came off herself in a launch and passed up a letter directed to the chief engineer. It reached him in the engine-room, where he, not knowing that she was but a few feet distant, was spared the sight of her pale and despairing face.

The letter itself was almost incoherent. She knew, she said, whom she had to thank for his departure. That vixen, that hussy, that stuck-up minx, who treated him like a dog and yet grudged him to another, who, God help her, loved him too well for her own good - it was her ladyship she had to thank for spoiling everything and carrying him away. Was he not man enough to assert himself and leave a ship where he was put upon so awful? Let him ask her mightiness in two words, yes or no; and then when he had come down from the clouds and had learned the truth, poor silly fool - then let him come back to his Cassie, who loved him so dear, and who (if she did say it herself) had a heart worth fifty of his mistress and didn't need no powder to set off her complexion. It ended with a piteous appeal to his compassion and besought him to write to her from the nearest port.

Frank sighed as he read it. Everything in the world seemed wrong and at cross-purposes. Those who had one thing invariably longed for something else, and there was no content or happiness or satisfaction anywhere. The better off were the acquiescent, who took the good and the bad with the same composure and found their only pleasure in their work. Best off of all were the dead whose sufferings were over. But after all it was sweet to be loved, even if one did not love back, and Frank was very tender with the little letter and put it carefully in his pocket-book. Yes, it was sweet to be loved. He said this over and over to himself, and wondered whether Florence felt the same to him as he did to Cassie. It seemed to explain so much. It seemed the key to her strange regard for him. He asked himself whether it could be true that she had wilfully ordered the ship to sea in order to prevent him going to the dance. The thought stirred him inexpressibly. What other explanation was there if this was not the one? And she had deserted the count, who was away in London on a day's business; deserted the Paquita at anchor in the roads! He was frightened at his own exultation. Suppose he were wrong in this surmise! Suppose it were just another of her unaccountable caprices!

They ran down Channel at full speed and at night were abreast of the Scilly lights, driving towards the Bay of Biscay in the teeth of an Equinoctial gale. At the behest of one girl eighty men had to endure the discomfort of a storm at sea, and a great steel ship, straining and quivering, was flung into the perilous night. It seemed a misuse of power that, at a woman's whim, so many lives and so noble and costly a fabric could be risked - and risked for nothing. From the captain on the bridge, dripping in his oil-skins, to the coal-passers and firemen below who fed the mighty furnaces, to the cooks in the galley, the engineers, the electrician on duty, the lookout man in the bow clinging to the life-line when the Minnehaha buried her nose out of sight - all these perforce had to endure and suffer at Florence's bidding without question or revolt.

Frank's elation passed and left him in a bitter humour towards her. It was not right, he said to himself, not right at all. She ought to show a little consideration for the men who had served her so well and faithfully.

Besides, it was unworthy of her to betray such pettiness and spoil Cassie's dance. He felt for the girl's humiliation, and, though not in love with her, he was conscious of a sentiment that hated to see her hurt. He would not accept Florence's invitation to dine in the saloon, sending word that he had a headache and begged to be excused; and after dinner, when she sought him out on deck and tried to make herself very sweet to him, he was purposely reserved and distant, and look the first opportunity to move away. He was angry, disheartened, and resentful, all in one.

Towards eleven o'clock at night as Frank was in the engine-room, moodily turning over these reflections in his mind and listening to the race of the screws as again and again they were lifted out of the water and strained the shafts and engines to the utmost, he was surprised to see Florence herself descending the steel ladder into that close atmosphere of oil and steam. He ran to help her down, and taking her arm led her to one side, where they might be out of the way. Here, in the glare of the lanterns, he looked down into her face and thought again how beautiful she was. Her cheek was wet with spray, and her hair was tangled and glistening beneath her little yachting cap. She seemed to exhale a breath of the storm above and bring down with her something of the gale itself. She held fast to Frank as the ship laboured and plunged, smiling as their eyes met.

"You are the last person I expected down here," said Frank.

"I was beginning to get afraid," she returned. "It's blowing terribly, Frank - and I thought, if anything happened, I'd like to be with you!"

"Oh, we are all right!" said Frank, his professional spirit aroused. "With twin screws, twin engines, and plenty of sea-room - why, let it blow."

His confidence reassured her. He never appeared to her so strong, so self-reliant and calm as at that moment of her incipient fear. Amongst his engines Frank always wore a masterful air, for he had that instinct for machinery peculiarly American, and was competent almost to the point of genius.

"Besides, I wanted to ask you a question," said Florence. "I had to ask it. I couldn't sleep without asking it, Frank."

"I would have come, if you had sent for me," he said.

"I couldn't wait for that," she returned. "I knew it might be hard for you to leave - or impossible."

"What is it, Florence?" he asked. The name slipped out in spite of him.

She looked at him strangely, her lustrous eyes wide open and bright with her unsaid thoughts.

"Are you very fond of her, Frank?" she asked.

"Her? Who?" he exclaimed. "You don't mean Cassie Derwent?"

"Yes," she said.

"Of course I'm fond of her," he said.

"More than you are of me, Frank?" she persisted.

"Oh, it isn't the same sort of thing, Florence," he said. "I never even thought of comparing you and her together. Surely you know that? Surely you understand that?"

"You used to - to love me once, Frank," she said, with a stifled sob. "Has she made it any less? Has she robbed me, Frank? Have I lost you without knowing it?"

"No," he said, "no, a thousand times, no!"

"Tell me that you love me, Frank," she burst out. "Tell me, tell me!" Then, as he did not answer, she went on passionately: "That's why I went to sea, Frank. I was mad with jealousy. I couldn't give you up to her. I couldn't let her have you!"

She pressed closer against him, and tiptoeing so as to raise her mouth to his ear, she whispered: "I always liked you better than anybody else in the world, Frank. I love you! I love you!"

For the moment he could not realise his own good fortune. He could do nothing but look into her eyes. It was her reproach for years afterwards that she had to kiss him first.

"I suppose it had to come, Frank," she said. "I fought all I could, but it didn't seem any use!"

"It was inevitable," he returned solemnly. "God made you for me, and me for you!"

"Amen," she said, and in an ecstasy of abandonment whispered again: "I love you, Frank. I love you!"

FFRENCHES FIRST

I suppose if I had been a hero of romance, instead of an ordinary kind of chap, I would have steamed in with the Tallahassee, fired a gun, and landed in state, instead of putting on my old clothes and sneaking into the county on an automobile. However, I did my little best, so far as making a date with Babcock was concerned, and as it turned out in the end I dare say the hero of romance wouldn't have managed it much better himself. It was late when I got into Forty Fyles (as the village was called), and put up at one of those quaint, low-raftered, bulging old inns which still remain, thank Heaven, here and there, in the less travelled parts of England. If I were dusty and dirty when I arrived, you ought to have seen me the next day after a two-hours' job with the differential gears. By the time I had got the trouble to rights, and had puffed up and down the main street to make assurance sure and astonish the natives (who came out two hundred strong and cheered), I was as frowsy, unkempt, and dilapidated an American as ever drove a twelve H.P. Panhard through the rural lanes of Britain. Indeed, I was so shocked at my own appearance when I looked at myself in the glass (such a wiggly old glass that showed one in streaks like bacon) that I went down to the draper's and tried to buy a new set out. But as they had nothing except cheap tripper suits for pigmies (I stood six feet in my stockings and had played full back at college)

Lloyd Osbourne

and fishermen's clothes of an ancient Dutch design, I forebore to waste my good dollars in making a guy of myself, and decided to remain as I was.

Then, as I was sitting in the bar and asking the potman the best way to get to Castle Fyles, it suddenly came over me that it was the Fourth of July, and that, recreant as I was, I had come near forgetting the event altogether. I started off again down the main street to discover some means of raising a noise, and after a good deal of searching I managed to procure several handfuls of strange whitey fire-crackers the size of cigars and a peculiar red package that the shopkeeper called a "Haetna Volcano." He said that for four and eightpence one couldn't find its match in Lunnon itself, and obligingly took off twopence when I pointed out Vesuvius hadn't a fuse. With the crackers in my pocket and the volcano under my arm I set forth in the pleasant summer morning to walk to Castle Fyles, having an idea to rest by the way and celebrate the Fourth in the very heart of the hereditary enemy.

The road, as is so often the case in England, ran between high stone walls and restrained the wayfarer from straying into the gentlemen's parks on either hand. The sun shone overhead with the fierce heat of a British July; and to make matters worse in my case, I seemed to be the loadstone of what traffic was in progress on the highway. A load of hay stuck to me with obstinate determination; if I walked slowly, the hay lagged beside me; if I quickened my pace, the hay whipped up his horses; when I rested and mopped my brow, the hay rested and mopped ITS brow. Then there were tramps of various kinds: a Punch and Judy show on the march; swift silent bicyclists who sped past in a flurry of dust; local gentry riding cock-horses (no doubt to Banbury Crosses); local gentry in dogcarts; local gentry in closed carriages going to a funeral, and apparently (as seen through the windows) very hot and mournful and perspiring; an antique clergyman in an antique gig who gave me a tract and warned me against drink; a char-a-bancs filled to bursting with the True Blue Constitutional Club of East Pigley - such at least was the inscription on a streaming banner - who swung past waving their hats and singing "Our Boarder's such a Nice Young Man"; then some pale aristocratic children in a sort of perambulating clothes-basket drawn by a hairy mite of a pony, who looked at me disapprovingly, as though I hadn't honestly come by the volcano; then - but why go on with the never-ending procession of British pilgrims who straggled out at just sufficient intervals to keep between them a perpetual eye on my movements and prevent me from celebrating the birth of freedom in any kind of privacy. At last, getting desperate at this espionage and thinking besides I could make a shorter cut towards Castle Fyles, I clambered over an easy place in the left-hand wall and dropped into the shade of a magnificent park. Here, at least, whatever the risk of an outraged law (which I had been patronisingly told was even stricter than that of the Medes and Persians), I seemed free to wander unseen and undetected, and accordingly struck a course under the oaks that promised in time to bring me out somewhere near the sea.

Dipping into a little dell, where in the perfection of its English woodland one might have thought to meet Robin Hood himself, or startle Little John beside a fallen deer, I looked carefully about, got out my pale crackers, and wondered whether I dared begin. It is always an eerie sensation to be alone in the forest, what with the whispering leaves overhead, the stir and hum of insects, the rustle of ghostly foot-falls, and (in my case) the uneasy sense of green-liveried keepers sneaking up at one through the clumps of gorse. However, I was not the man to belie the blood of Revolutionary heroes and meanly carry my unexploded crackers beyond the scene of danger, so I remembered the brave days of old and touched a whitey off. It burst with the roar of a cannon and reverberated through the glades like the broadside of a man-of-war. It took me a good five minutes before I had the courage to detonate another, which, for better security, I did this time under my hat. I am not saying it did the hat any good, but it seemed safer and less deafening, and I accordingly went on in this manner until there were only about three whiteys left between me and Vesuvius, which I kept back, in accordance with tradition, for one big triumphant bang at the end.

I was in the act of touching my cigar to whitey number three, - on my knees, I remember; and trying to arrange my hat so as to get the most muffling for the least outlay of burned felt, when the branches in front of me parted and I looked up to see - well, simply the most beautiful woman in the world, regarding me with astonishment and anger. She was about twenty, somewhat above the medium height, and her eyes were of a lovely flashing blue that seemed in the intensity of her indignation to positively emit sparks - altogether the most exquisitely radiant and glorious creature that man was ever privileged to gaze upon.

"How dare you let off fireworks in this park?" she said, in a voice like clotted cream.

I rose in some confusion.

"Go directly," she said, "or I'll report you and have you summonsed!"

"I have only two more crackers and this volcano," I said protestingly. "Surely you would not mind -"

"Don't be insolent," she said, "or I shall have no compunction in setting my dog on you."

I looked down, and there, sure enough, rolling a yellow eye and showing his fangs at me, was a sort of Uncle Tom's Cabin bloodhound only waiting to begin.

"The fact is," I said, speaking slowly, so as to emphasise the fact that I was a gentleman, "I am an American; to-day is our national holiday; and we make it everywhere our practice to celebrate it with fire-works. I would have done so in the road, but the island seemed so crowded this morning I couldn't find an undisturbed place outside the park."

Beauty was obviously mollified by my tone and respectful address.

"Please leave the park directly," she said.

I put the crackers in my pocket, took up my hat, placed the Haetna Volcano under my arm, and stood there, ready to go.

"Accept my apologies," I said. "Whatever my fault, at least no discourtesy was intended."

We looked at each other, and Beauty's face relaxed into something like a smile.

"Just give me one more minute for my volcano," I pleaded.

"You seem very polite," she returned. "Yes, you can set it off, if that will be any satisfaction to you."

"It'll be a whole lot," I said, "and since you're so kind perhaps you'll let me include the crackers as well?"

Then she began to laugh, and the sweetest thing about it was that she didn't want to laugh a bit and blushed the most lovely pink, as she broke out again and again until the woods fairly rang. And as I laughed too - for really it was most absurd - it was as good as a scene in a play. And so, while she held Legree's dog, whom the sound inflamed to frenzy, I popped off the crackers and dropped my cigar into Vesuvius. I tell you he was worth four and eightpence, and the man was right when he said there wasn't his match in London. I doubt if there was his match anywhere for being plumb-full of red balls and green balls and blue balls and crimson stars and fizzlegigs and whole torrents of tiny crackers and chase-me-quicks, and when you about thought he was never going to stop he shot up a silver spray and a gold spray and wound up with a very considerable decent-sized bust.

"I must thank you for your good nature," I said to the young lady.

"Are you a typical American?" she asked. "Oh, so-so," I returned. "There are heaps like me in New York."

"And do they all do this on the Fourth of July?" she asked.

"Every last one!" I said.

"Fancy!" she said.

"In America," I said, "when a man has received one favour he is certain to make it the stepping-stone for another. Won't you permit me to walk across the park to Castle Fyles?"

"Castle Fyles?" she repeated, with a little note of curiosity in her girlish voice. "Then don't you know that this is Fyles Park?"

"Can't say I did," I returned. "But I am delighted to hear it."

"Why are you delighted to hear it?" she asked, making me feel more than ever like an escaped lunatic.

"This is the home of my ancestors," I said, "and it makes me glad to think they amount to something - own real estate - and keep their venerable heads above water."

"So this is the home of your ancestors," she said.

"It's holy ground to me," I said.

"Fancy!" she exclaimed.

"At least I think it is," I went on, "though we haven't any proofs beyond the fact that Fyles has always been a family name with us back to the Colonial days. I'm named Fyles myself - Fyles ffrench - and we, like the Castle people - have managed to retain our little f throughout the ages."

She looked at me so incredulously that I handed her my card.

Mr. Fyles ffrench,

Knickerbocker Club.

She turned it over in her fingers, regarding me at the same time with flattering curiosity.

"How do you do, kinsman?" she said, holding out her hand. "Welcome to old England!"

I took her little hand and pressed it.

"I am the daughter of the house," she explained, "and I'm named Fyles too, though they usually call me Verna."

"And the little f, of course," I said.

"Just like yours," she returned. "There may be some capital F's in the family, but we wouldn't acknowledge them!"

"What a fellow-feeling that gives one!" I said. "At school, at college, in business, in the war with Spain when I served on the Dixie, my life has been one long struggle to preserve that little f against a capital F world. I remember saying that to a chum the day we sank Cervera, 'If I am killed, Bill,' I said, 'see that they don't capital F me on the scroll of fame!'"

"A true ffrench!" exclaimed Beauty with approval.

"As true as yourself," I said.

"Do you know that I'm the last of them?" she said.

"You!" I exclaimed. "The last!"

"Yes," she said, "when my father dies the estates will pass to my second cousin, Lord George Willoughby, and our branch of the family will become extinct."

"You fill me with despair," I said.

"My father never can forgive me for being a girl," she said.

"I can," I remarked, "even at the risk of appearing disloyal to the race."

"Fyles," she said, addressing me straight out by my first name, and with a little air that told me plainly I had made good my footing in the fold, "Fyles, what a pity you aren't the rightful heir, come from overseas with parchments and parish registers, to make good your claim before the House of Lords."

"Wouldn't that be rather hard on you?" I asked.

"I'd rather give up everything than see the old place pass to strangers," she said.

"But I'm a stranger," I said.

"You're Fyles ffrench," she exclaimed, "and a man, and you'd hand the old name down and keep the estate together."

"And guard the little f with the last drop of my blood," I said.

"Ah, well!" she said, with a little sigh, "the world's a disappointing place at best, and I suppose it serves us right for centuries of conceit about ourselves."

"That at least will never die," I observed. "The American branch will see to that part of it."

"It's a pity, though, isn't it?" she said.

"Well," I said, "when a family has been carrying so much dog for a thousand years, I suppose in common fairness it's time to give way for another."

"What is carrying dog?" she said.

"It's American," I returned, "for thinking yourself better than anybody else!"

"Fancy!" she said, and then with a beautiful smile she took my hand and rubbed it against the hound's muzzle.

"You mustn't growl at him, Olaf," she said. "He's a ffrench; he's one of us; and he has come from over the sea to make friends."

"You can't turn me out of the park after that," I said, in spite of a very dubious lick from the noble animal, who, possibly because he couldn't read and hadn't seen my card, was s till a prey to suspicion.

"I am going to take you back to the castle myself," she said, "and we'll spend the day going all over it, and I shall introduce you to my father - Sir Fyles - when he returns at five from Ascot."

"I could ask for nothing better," I said, "though I don't want to make myself a burden to you. And then," I went on, a little uncertain how best to express myself, "you are so queer in England about - about -"

"Proprieties," she said, giving the word which I hesitated to use. "Oh, yes! I suppose I oughtn't to; indeed, it's awful, and there'll be lunch too, Fyles, which makes it twice as bad. But to-day I'm going to be American and do just what I like."

"I thought I ought to mention it," I said.

"Objection overruled," she returned. "That's what they used to say in court when my father had his famous right-of-way case with Lord Piffle of Doom; and from what I remember there didn't seem any repartee to it."

"There certainly isn't one from me," I said.

"Let's go," she said.

There didn't seem any end to that park, and we walked and walked and rested once or twice under the deep shade, and took in a mouldy pavilion in white marble with broken windows, and a Temple of Love that dated back to the sixteenth century, and rowed on an ornamental water in a real gondola that leaked like sixty, and landed on a rushy island where there was a sun-dial and a stone seat that the Druids or somebody had considerately placed there in the year one, and talked of course, and grew confidential, until finally I was calling her Verna (which was her pet name) and telling her how the other fellow had married my best girl, while she spoke most beautifully and sensibly about love, and the way the old families were dying out because they had set greater store on their lands than on their hearts, and altogether with what she said and what I said, and what was understood, we passed from acquaintance to friendship, and from friendship to the verge of something even nearer. Even the Uncle Tom hound fell under the spell of our new-found intimacy and condescended to lick my hand of his own volition, which Verna said he had never done before except to the butcher, and winked a bloodshot eye when I remarked he was too big for the island and ought to go back with me to a country nearer his size.

By the time we had reached the cliffs and began to perceive the high grey walls of the castle in the distance, Verna and I were faster friends than ever, and anyone seeing us together would have thought we had known each other all our lives. I felt more and more happy to think I had met her first in this unconventional way, for as the castle loomed up closer and we passed gardeners and keepers and jockeys with a string of race-horses out for exercise, I felt that my pretty companion was constrained by the sight of these obsequious faces and changing by gradations into what she really was, the daughter of the castle and by right of blood one of the great ladies of the countryside.

The castle itself was a tremendous old pile, built on a rocky peninsula and surrounded on three sides by the waters of Appledore Harbour, It lay so as to face the entrance, which Verna told me was commanded - or rather had been in years past - by the guns of a half-moon battery that stood planted on a sort of third-story terrace. It was all towers and donjons and ramparts, and might, in its mediaeval perfection, have been taken bodily out of one of Sir Walter Scott's novels. Verna and I had lunch together in a perfectly gorgeous old hall, with beams and carved panelling and antlers, and a fireplace you could have roasted an ox in, and rows of glistening suits of armour which the original ffrenches had worn when they had first started the family in life - and all this, if you please, tete-a-tete with a woman who seemed to get more beautiful every minute I gazed at her, and who smiled back at me and called me Fyles, to the stupefaction of three noiseless six-footers in silk stockings. Disapproving six-footers, too, whose gimlet eyes seemed to pierce my back as they sized up my clothes, which, as I said before, had suffered not a little by my trip, and my collar, which I'll admit straight out wasn't up to a castle standard, and the undeniable stain of machine-oil on my cuffs which I had got that morning in putting the machine to rights. You ought to have seen the man that took my hat, which he did with the air of a person receiving pearls and diamonds on a golden platter, and smudged his lordly fingers with the grime of my Fourth of July. And that darling of a girl, who never noticed my discomfiture, but whose eyes sparkled at times with a hidden merriment - shall I ever forget her as she sat there and helped me to mutton-chops from simply priceless old Charles the First plate!

We had black coffee together in a window-seat overlooking the harbour and the ships, and she asked me a lot of questions about the war with Spain and my service in the Dixie. She never moved a muscle when it came out I had been a quartermaster, though I could feel she was astounded at my being but a shade above a common seaman, and not, as she had taken it for granted, a commissioned officer. I was too proud to explain over-much, or to tell her I had gone in, as so many of my friends had done, from a strong sense of duty and patriotism at the time of my country's need, and consequently allowed her to get a very wrong idea, I suppose, about my state in life and position in the world. Indeed, I was just childish enough to get a trifle wounded, and let her add misconception to misconception out of a silly obstinacy.

"But what do you do," she asked, "now that the war is over and you've taken away everything from the poor Spaniards and left the Navy?"

"Work," I said.

"What kind of work?" she asked.

"Oh, in an office!" I said. (I didn't tell her I was the Third Vice President of the Amalgamated Copper Company, with a twenty-story building on lower Broadway. Wild horses couldn't have wrung it out of me then.)

"You're too nice for an office," she said, looking at me so sweetly and sadly. "You ought to be a gentleman!"

"Oh, dear!" I exclaimed, "I hope I am that, even if I do grub along in an office." I wish my partners could have heard me say that. Why, I have a private elevator of my own and a squash-court on the roof!

"Of course, I don't mean that," she went on quickly, "but like us, I mean, with a castle and a place in society -"

"I have a sort of little picayune place in New York," I interrupted. "I don't SLEEP in the office, you know. At night I go out and see my friends and sometimes they invite me to dinner."

She looked at me more sadly than ever. I don't believe humour was Verna's strong suit anyway, - not American humour, at least, - for she not only believed what I said, but more too.

"I must speak to Papa about you," she said.

"What will he do?" I asked.

"Oh, help you along, you know," she said; "ffrenches always stand together; it's a family trait, though it's dying out now for lack of ffrenches. You know our family motto?" she went on.

"I'm afraid I don't," I said.

"'Ffrenches first!'" she returned.

I had to laugh.

"We've lived up to it in America," I said.

"Papa is quite a power in the City," she said.

"I thought he was a gentleman," I replied.

"Everybody dabbles in business nowadays," she returned, not perceiving the innuendo. "I am sure Papa ought to know all about it from the amount of money he has lost."

"Perhaps his was a case of ffrenches last!" I said.

"Still, he knows all the influential people," she continued, "and it would be so easy for him to get you a position over here."

"That would be charming," I said.

"And then I might see you occasionally," she said, with such a little ring of kindness in her voice that for a minute I felt a perfect brute for deceiving her. "You could run down here from Saturday to Monday, you know, and on Bank Holidays, and in the season you would have the entree to our London house and the chance of meeting nice people!"

"How jolly!" I said.

"I can't bear you to go back to America," she said. "Now that I've found you, I'm going to keep you."

"I hate the thought of going back myself," I said, and so I did - at the thought of leaving that angel!

"Then, you know," she went on, somewhat shyly and hesitatingly, "you have such good manners and such a good air, and you're so -"

"Don't mind saying handsome," I remarked.

"You really are very nice-looking," she said, with a seriousness that made me acutely uncomfortable, "and what with our friendship and our house open to you and the people you could invite down here, because I know Papa is going to go out of his mind about you - he and I are always crazy about the same people, you know - not to speak of the little f, there is no reason, Fyles, why in the end you shouldn't marry an awfully rich girl and set up for yourself!"

"Thank you," I said, "but if it's all the same to you I don't think I'd care to."

"I know awfully rich girls who are pretty too," she said, as though forestalling an objection.

"I do too," I said, looking at her so earnestly that she coloured up to the eyes.

"Oh, I am poor!" she said. "It's all we can do to keep the place up. Besides - besides -" And then she stopped and looked out of the window. I saw I had been a fool to be so personal, and I was soon punished for my presumption, for she rose to her feet and said in an altered voice that she would now show me the castle.

As I said before, it was a tremendous old place. It was a two-hours' job to go through it even as we did, and then Verna said we had skipped a whole raft of things she would let me see some other time. There was a private theatre, a chapel with effigies of cross-legged Crusaders, an armoury with a thousand stand of flint-locks, a library, magnificent state apartments with wonderful tapestries, a suite of rooms where they had confined a mad ffrench in the fifteenth century, with the actual bloodstains on the floor where he had dashed out his poor silly brains against the wall; a magazine with a lot of empty powder-casks Cromwell had left there; a vaulted chamber for the men of the half-moon battery; a well which was said to have no bottom and which had remained unused for a hundred years, because a wicked uncle had thrown the rightful heir into it; and slimy, creepy-crawly dungeons with chains for your hands and feet; and cachettes where they spilled you through a hole in the floor, and let it go at that; and - but what wasn't there, indeed, in that extraordinary old feudal citadel, which had been in continuous human possession since the era of Hardicanute. There seemed to be only one thing missing in the whole castle, and that was a bath - though I dare say there was one in the private apartments not shown to me. It was a regular dive into the last five hundred years, and the fact that it wasn't a museum nor exploited by a sing-song cicerone, helped to make it for me a memorable and really thrilling experience. I conjured up my forebears and could see them playing as children, growing to manhood, passing into old age, and finally dying in the shadow of those same massive walls. Verna said I was quite pale when we emerged at last into the open air on the summit of the high square tower; and no wonder that I was, for in a kind of way I had been deeply impressed, and it seemed a solemn thing that I, like her, should be a child of this castle, with roots deep cast in far-off ages.

"Wouldn't it be horrible," I said, "if I found out I wasn't a ffrench at all - but had really sprung from a low-down, capital F family in the next county or somewhere!"

"Oh, but you are a real ffrench," said Verna.

"How do you know?" I asked.

"I can FEEL it," she said. "I never felt that kind of sensation before towards anybody except my father!"

I hardly knew whether to be pleased or not. And besides, it didn't seem to me conclusive.

Then she touched a button (for the castle was thoroughly wired and there was even a miniature telephone system) and servants brought us up afternoon tea, and a couple of chairs to sit on, and a folding table set out with flowers, and the best toast and the best tea and the best strawberry jam and the best chocolate cake and the best butter that I had as yet tasted in the whole island. The view itself was good enough to eat, for we were high above everything and saw the harbour and the country stretched out on all sides like a map.

"This is where I come for my day-dreams," said Verna. "I usually have it all to myself, for people hate the stairs so much and the ladies twitter about the dust and the cobwebs and the shakiness of the last ladder, and the silly things get dizzy and have to be held."

"You don't seem to be afraid," I said.

"This has been my favourite spot all my life," she returned. "I can remember Papa holding me up when I wasn't five years old and telling me about the Lady Grizzle that threw herself off the parapet rather than marry somebody she had to and wouldn't!"

"Tell me about your day-dreams, Verna," I said.

"Just a girl's fancies," she returned, smiling. "I dare say men have them too. Fairy princes, you know, and what he'd say and what I'd say, and how much I'd love him, and how much he'd love me!"

"I can understand the last part of it," I observed.

"You are really very nice," she returned, "and when Papa has got you that place in the City, I am going to allow you to come up here and dream too. And you'll tell me about the Sleeping Beauty and I'll unbosom myself about the Beast, and we'll exchange heart-aches and be, oh, so happy together."

"I am that now," I said.

"You're awfully easily pleased, Fyles," she said. "Most of the men I know I have to rack my head to entertain; talk exploring, you know, to explorers, and horses to Derby winners, and what it feels like to be shot - to soldiers - but you entertain ME, and that is so much pleasanter."

"I wish I dared ask you some questions," I said.

"Oh, but you mustn't!" she broke out, with a quick intuition of what I meant.

"Why mustn't?" T asked.

"Oh, because - because -" she returned. "I wouldn't like to fib to you, and I wouldn't like to tell you the truth - and it would make me feel hot and uncomfortable -"

"What would?" I asked.

"You see, if I really cared for him, it would be different," she said. "But I don't - and that's all."

"Lady Grizzle over again?" I ventured.

"Not altogether," she said, "you see she was perfectly mad about somebody else - which really was hard lines for her, poor thing - while I -"

"Oh, please go on!" I said, as she hesitated.

"Fyles," she said, with the ghost of a sigh, "this isn't day-dreaming at all, and I'm going to give you another cup of tea and change the subject."

"What would you prefer, then?" I asked. "No! No more chocolate cake, thank you."

"Let's have a fairy story all of our own," she said.

"Well, you begin," I said.

"Once upon a time," she began, "there was a poor young man in New York - an American, though of course he couldn't help that - and he came over to England and discovered the home of his ancestors, and he liked them, and they liked him - ever so much, you know - and he found that the old place was destined to pass to strangers, and so he worked and worked in a dark old office, and stayed up at night working some more, and never accepted any invitations or took a holiday except at week-ends to the family castle - until finally he amassed an immense fortune. Then he got into a fairy chariot, together with a bag of gold and the family lawyer, and ordered the coachman to drive him to Lord George Willoughby's in Curzon Street. Then they sent out in hot haste for Sir George's son, an awfully fast young man in the Guards, and the family lawyer haggled and haggled, and Lord George hemmed and hawed, and the Guardsman's eyes sparkled with greed at the sight of the bag of gold, and finally for two hundred thousand pounds (Papa says he often thinks he could pull it off for a hundred and ten thousand) the entail is broken and everybody signs his name to the papers and the poor young man buys the succession of Fyles and comes down here, regardless of expense, in a splendid gilt special train, and is received with open arms by his kinsmen at the castle."

"The open arms appeal to me," I said.

"He was nearly hugged to death," said Verna, "for they were so pleased the old name was not to die out and be forgotten. And then the poor young man married a ravishing beauty and had troops of sunny-haired children, and the daughter of the castle (who by this time was an old maid and quite plain, though everybody said she had a heart like hidden treasure) devoted herself to the little darlings and taught them music-lessons and manners and how to spell their names with a little f, and as a great treat would sometimes bring them up here and tell them how she had first met the poor young man in the 'diamond mornings of long ago'!"

"That's a good fairy story," I said, "but you are all out about the end!"

"You said you liked it," she protested.

"Yes, where they hugged the poor young man," I returned, "but after that, Verna, it went off the track altogether."

"Perhaps you'll put it back again," she said.

"I want to correct all that about the daughter of the castle," I said. "She never became an old maid at all, for, of course, the poor young man loved her to distraction and married her right off, and they lived happily together ever afterwards!"

"I believe that is nicer," she said thoughtfully, as though considering the matter.

"Truer, too," I said, "because really the poor young man adored her from the first minute of their meeting!"

"I wonder how long it will take him to make his fortune," she said, which, under the circumstances, struck me as a cruel thing to say.

"Possibly he has made it already," I said. "How do you know he hasn't?"

"By his looks for one thing," she said, regarding the machine oil on my cuff out of the corner of her eye. "Besides, he hasn't any of the arrogance of a parvenu, and is much too -"

"Too what?" I asked.

"Well bred," she replied simply.

"No doubt that's the ffrench in him," I said, which I think was rather a neat return.

She didn't answer, but looked absently across to the harbour mouth.

"I believe there is a steamer coming in," she said. "Yes, a steamer."

"A yacht, I think," I said, for, sure enough, it was Babcock true to the minute, heading the Tallahassee straight in. I could have given him a hundred dollars on the spot I was so delighted, for he couldn't have timed it better, nor at a moment when it could have pleased me more. She ran in under easy steam, making a splendid appearance with her raking masts and razor bow, under which the water spurted on either side like dividing silver. Except a beautiful woman, I don't know that there's a sweeter sight than a powerful, sea-going steam yacht, with the sun glinting on her bright brass-work, and a uniformed crew jumping to the sound of the boatswain's whistle.

"The poor young man's ship's come home," I said.

"It must be Lady Gaunt's Sapphire," said Verna.

"With the American colours astern?" I said.

"Why, how strange," she said, "it really is American. And then I believe it's larger than the Sapphire!"

"Fifteen hundred and four tons register," I said.

"How do you know that?" she demanded, with a shade of surprise in her voice.

"Because, my dear, it's mine!" I said.

"Yours!" she cried out in astonishment.

"If you doubt me," I said, "I shall tell you what she is going to do next. She is about to steam in here and lower a boat to take me aboard."

"She's heading for Dartmouth," said Verna incredulously, and the words were hardly out of her pretty mouth when Babcock swung round and pointed the Tallahassee's nose straight at us.

For a moment Verna was too overcome to speak.

"Fyles," she said at last, "you told me you worked in an office!"

"So I do," I said.

"And own a vessel like that!" she exclaimed. "A yacht the size of a man-of-war!"

"It was you that said I was a poor young man," I observed. "I was so pleased at being called young that I let the poor pass."

"Fancy!" she exclaimed, looking at me with eyes like stars. And then, recovering herself, she added in another tone: "Now don't you think it was very forward to rendezvous at a private castle?"

"Oh, I thought I could make myself solid before she arrived," I said.

"Fyles," she said, "I am beginning to have a different opinion of you. You are not as straightforward as a ffrench ought to be - and, though I'm ashamed to say it of you - but you are positively conceited."

"Unsay, take back, those angry words," I said; and even as I did so the anchor went splash and I could hear the telegraph jingle in the engine-room.

"And so you're rich," said Verna, "awfully, immensely, disgustingly rich, and you've been masquerading all this afternoon as a charming pauper!"

"I don't think I said charming," I remarked.

"But I say it," said Verna, "because, really you know, you're awfully nice, and I like you, and I'm glad from the bottom of my heart that you are rich!"

"Thank you," I said, "I'm glad, too."

"Now we must go down and meet your boat," said Verna. "See, there it is, coming in - though I still think it was cheeky of you to tell them to land uninvited."

"Oh, let them wait!" I said.

"No, no, we must go and meet them," said Verna, "and I'm going to ask that glorious old fox with the yellow beard whether it's all true or not!"

"You can't believe it yet?" I said.

"You've only yourself to thank for it," she said. "I got used to you as one thing - and here you are, under my eyes, turning out another."

I could not resist saying "Fancy!" though she did not seem to perceive any humour in my exclamation of it, and took it as a matter of course. Besides, she had risen now, and bade me follow her down the stairs.

It was really fine to see the men salute me as we walked down to the boat, and the darkies' teeth shining at the sight of me (for I'm a believer in the coloured sailor) and old Neilsen grinning respectfully in the stern-sheets.

"Neilsen," I said, "tell this young lady my name!"

"Mr. ffrench, sir," he answered, considerably astonished at the question.

"Little f or big F, Neilsen?"

"Little f, sir," said Neilsen.

"There, doubter!" I said to Verna.

She had her hand on my arm and was smiling down at the men from the little stone pier on which we stood.

"Fyles," she said, "you must land and dine with us to-night, not only because I want you to, but because you ought to meet my father."

"About when?" I asked.

"Seven-thirty," she answered; and then, in a lower voice, so that the men below might not hear: "Our fairy tale is coming true, isn't it, Fyles?"

"Right to the end," I said.

"There were two ends," she said. "Mine and yours."

"Oh, mine," I said; "that is, if you'll live up to your part of it!"

"What do you want me to do?" she asked.

"Throw over the Beast and be my Princess," I said, trying to talk lightly, though my voice betrayed me.

"Perhaps I will," she answered.

"Perhaps!" I repeated. "That isn't any answer at all."

"Yes, then!" she said quickly, and, disengaging her hand from my arm, ran back a few steps.

"I hear Papa's wheels," she cried over her shoulder, "and, don't forget, Fyles, dinner at seven-thirty!"

Lloyd Osbourne

THE GOLDEN CASTAWAYS

All I did was to pull him out by the seat of the trousers. The fat old thing had gone out in the dark to the end of the yacht's boat-boom, and was trying to worry in the dinghy with his toe, when plump he dropped into a six-knot ebb tide. Of course, if I hadn't happened along in a launch, he might have drowned, but, as for anything heroic on my part - why, the very notion is preposterous. The whole affair only lasted half a minute, and in five he was aboard his yacht and drinking hot Scotch in a plush dressing-gown. It was natural that his wife and daughter should be frightened, and natural, too, I suppose, that when they had finished crying over him they should cry over me. He had taken a chance with the East River, and it had been the turn of a hair whether he floated down the current a dead grocer full of brine, or stood in that cabin, a live one full of grog. Oh, no! I am not saying a word against THEM. But as for Grossensteck himself, he ought really to have known better, and it makes me flush even now to recall his monstrous perversion of the truth. He called me a hero to my face. He invented details to which my dry clothes gave the lie direct. He threw fits of gratitude. His family were theatrically commanded to regard me well, so that my countenance might be forever imprinted on their hearts; and they, poor devils, in a seventh heaven to have him back safe and sound in their midst, regarded and regarded, and imprinted and imprinted, till I felt like a perfect ass masquerading as a Hobson.

It was all I could do to tear myself away. Grossensteck clung to me. Mrs. Grossensteck clung to me. Teresa - that was the daughter - Teresa, too, clung to me. I had to give my address. I had to take theirs. Medals were spoken of; gold watches with inscriptions; a common purse, on which I was requested to confer the favour ofdrawing for the term of my natural life. I departed in a blaze of glory, and though I could not but see the ridiculous side of the affair (I mean as far as I was concerned), I was moved by so affecting a family scene, and glad, indeed, to think that the old fellow had been spared to his wife and daughter. I had even a pang of envy, for I could not but contrast myself with Grossensteck, and wondered if there were two human beings in the world who would have cared a snap whether I lived or died. Of course, that was just a passing mood, for, as a matter of fact, I am a man with many friends, and I knew some would feel rather miserable were I to make a hole in saltwater. But, you see, I had just had a story refused by Schoonmaker's Magazine, a good story, too, and that always gives me a sinking feeling - to think that after all these years I am still on the borderland of failure, and can never be sure of acceptance, even by the second-class periodicals for which I write. However, in a day or two, I managed to unload "The Case against Phillpots" on somebody else, and off I started for the New Jersey coast with a hundred and fifty dollars in my pocket, and no end of plans for a long autumn holiday.

I never gave another thought to Grossensteck until one morning, as I was sitting on the veranda of my boarding-house, the postman appeared and requested me to sign for a registered package. I opened it with some trepidation, for I had caught that fateful name written crosswise in the corner and began at once to apprehend the worst. I think I have as much assurance as any man, but it took all I had and more, too, when I unwrapped a gold medal the thickness and shape of an enormous checker, and deciphered the following inscription:

Presented to Hugo Dundonald Esquire for having With signal heroism, gallantry and presence of mind rescued On the night of June third, 1900 the life of Hermann Grossensteck from The dark and treacherous waters of the East River.

The thing was as thick as two silver dollars, laid the one on the other, and gold - solid, ringing, massy gold - all the way through; and it was associated with a blue satin ribbon, besides, which was to serve for sporting it on my manly bosom. I set it on the rail and laughed - laughed till the tears ran down my cheeks - while the other boarders crowded about me; handed it from hand to hand; grew excited to think that they had a hero in their midst; and put down my explanation to the proverbial modesty of the brave. Blended with my amusement were some qualms at the intrinsic value of the medal, for it could scarcely have cost less than three or four hundred dollars, and it worried me to think that Grossensteck must have drawn so lavishly on his savings. It had not occurred to me, either before or then, that he was rich; somehow, in the bare cabin of the schooner, I had received no such impression of his means. I had not even realised that the vessel was his own, taking it for granted that it had been hired, all standing, for a week or two with the put-by economies of a year. His home address ought to have set me right, but I had not taken the trouble to read it, slipping it into my pocket-book more to oblige him than with any idea of following up the acquaintance. It was one of the boarders that enlightened me.

"Grossensteck!" he exclaimed; "why, that's the great cheap grocer of New York, the Park & Tilford of the lower orders! There are greenbacks in his rotten tea, you know, and places to leave your baby while you buy his sanded sugar, and if you save eighty tags of his syrup you get a silver spoon you wouldn't be found dead with! Oh, everybody knows Grossensteck!"

"Well, I pulled the great cheap grocer out of the East River," I said. "There was certainly a greenback in that tea," and I took another look at my medal, and began to laugh all over again.

"There's no reason why you should ever have another grocery bill," said the boarder. "That is, if flavour cuts no figure with you, and you'd rather eat condemned army stores than not!"

I sat down and wrote a letter of thanks. It was rather a nice letter, for I could not but feel pleased at the old fellow's gratitude, even if it were a trifle overdone, and, when all's said, it was undoubtedly a fault on the right side. I disclaimed the heroism, and bantered him good-naturedly about the medal, which, of course, I said I would value tremendously and wear on appropriate occasions. I wondered at the time what occasion could be appropriate to decorate one's self with a gold saucer covered with lies - but, naturally, I didn't go into that to HIM. When you accept a solid chunk of gold you might as well be handsome about it, and I piled it on about his being long spared to his family and to a world that wouldn't know how to get along without him. Yes, it was a stunning letter, and I've often had the pleasure of reading it since in a splendid frame below my photograph.

I had been a month or more in New York, and December was already well advanced before I looked up my Grossenstecks, which I did one late afternoon as I happened to be passing in their direction. It was a house of forbidding splendour, on the Fifth Avenue side of Central Park, and, as I trod its marble halls, I could not but repeat to myself: "Behold, the grocer's dream!" But I could make no criticism of my reception by Mrs. Grossensteck and Teresa, whom I found at home and delighted to see me. Mrs. Grossensteck was a stout, jolly, motherly woman, common, of course, - but, if you can understand what I mean, - common in a nice way, and honest and unpretentious and likable. Teresa, whom I had scarcely noticed on the night of the accident, was a charmingly pretty girl of eighteen, very chic and gay, with pleasant manners and a contagious laugh. She had arrived at obviously the turn of the Grossensteck fortunes, and might, in refinement and everything else, have belonged to another clay. How often one sees that in America, the land above others of social contrast, where, in the same family, there are often three separate degrees of caste.

Well, to get along with my visit. I liked them and they liked me, and I returned later the same evening to dine and meet papa. I found him as impassionedly grateful as before, and with a tale that trespassed even further on the incredible, and after dinner we all sat around a log fire and talked ourselves into a sort of intimacy.

They were wonderfully good people, and though we hadn't a word in common, nor an idea, we somehow managed to hit it off, as one often can with those who are unaffectedly frank and simple. I had to cry over the death of little Hermann in the steerage (when they had first come to America twenty years ago), and how Grossensteck had sneaked gingersnaps from the slop-baskets of the saloon.

"The little teffil never knew where they come from," said Grossensteck, "and so what matters it?"

"That's Papa's name in the slums," said Teresa. "Uncle Gingersnaps, because at all his stores they give away so many for nothing."

"By Jove!" I said, "there are some nick-names that are patents of nobility."

What impressed me as much as anything with these people was their loneliness. Parvenus are not always pushing and self-seeking, nor do they invariably throw down the ladder by which they have climbed. The Grossenstecks would have been so well content to keep their old friends, but poverty hides its head from the glare of wealth and takes fright at altered conditions.

"They come - yes," said Mrs. Grossensteck, "but they are scared of the fine house, of the high-toned help, of everything being gold, you know, and fashionable. And when Papa sends their son to college, or gives the girl a little stocking against her marriage day, they slink away ashamed. Oh, Mr. Dundonald, but it's hard to thank and be thanked, especially when the favours are all of one side!"

"The rich have efferyting," said Grossensteck, "but friends - Nein!"

New ones had apparently never come to take the places of the old; and the old had melted away. Theirs was a life of solitary grandeur, varied with dinner parties to their managers and salesmen. Socially speaking, their house was a desert island, and they themselves three castaways on a golden rock, scanning the empty seas for a sail. To carry on a metaphor, I might say I was the sail and welcomed accordingly. I was everything that they were not; I was poor; I mixed with people whose names filled them with awe; my own was often given at first nights and things of that sort. In New York, the least snobbish of great cities, a man need have but a dress suit and car-fare - if he be the right kind of a man, of course - to go anywhere and hold up his head with the best. In a place so universally rich, there is even a certain piquancy in being a pauper. The Grossenstecks were overcome to think I shined my own shoes, and had to calculate my shirts, and the fact that I was no longer young (that's the modern formula for forty), and next-door to a failure in the art I had followed for so many years, served to whet their pity and their regard. My little trashy love-stories seemed to them the fruits of genius, and they were convinced, the poor simpletons, that the big magazines were banded in a conspiracy to block my way to fame.

"My dear poy," said Grossensteck, "you know as much of peeziness as a child unporne, and I tell you it's the same efferywhere - in groceries, in hardware, in the alkali trade, in effery branch of industry, the pig operators stand shoulder to shoulder to spiflicate the little fellers like you. You must combine with the other producers; you must line up and break through the ring; you must scare them out of their poots, and, by Gott, I'll help you do it!"

In their naive interest in my fortunes, the Grossenstecks rejoiced at an acceptance, and were correspondingly depressed at my failures. A fifteen-dollar poem would make them happy for a week; and when some of my editors were slow to pay-on the literary frontiers there is a great deal of this sort of procrastination - Uncle Gingersnaps was always hot to put the matter into the hands of his collectors, and commence legal proceedings in default.

Little by little I drifted into a curious intimacy with the Grossenstecks. Their house by degrees became my refuge. I was given my own suite of rooms, my own latch-key; I came and went unremarked; and what I valued most of all was that my privacy was respected, and no one thought to intrude upon me when I closed my door. In time I managed to alter the whole house to my liking, and spent their money like water in the process. Gorgeousness gave way to taste; I won't be so fatuous as to say my taste; but mine was in conjunction with the best decorators in New York. One was no longer blinded by magnificence, but found rest and peace and beauty. Teresa and I bought the pictures. She was a wonderfully clever girl, full of latent appreciation and understanding which until then had lain dormant in her breast. I quickened those unsus-pected fires, and, though I do not vaunt my own judgment as anything extraordinary, it represented at least the conventional standard and was founded on years of observation and training. We let the old masters go as something too smudgy and recondite for any but experts, learning our lesson over one Correggio which nearly carried us into the courts, and bought modern American instead, amongst them some fine examples of our best men. We had a glorious time doing it, too, and showered the studios with golden rain - in some where it was evidently enough needed.

There was something childlike in the Grossenstecks' confidence in me; I mean the old people; for it was otherwise with Teresa, with whom I often quarrelled over my artistic reforms, and who took any conflict in taste to heart. There were whole days when she would not speak to me at all, while I, on my side, was equally obstinate, and all this, if you please, about some miserable tapestry or a Louise Seize chair or the right light for a picture of Will Low's. But she was such a sweet girl and so pretty that one could not be angry with her long, and what with our fights and our makings up I dare say we made it more interesting to each other than if we had always agreed. It was only once that our friendship was put in real jeopardy, and that was when her parents decided they could not die happy unless we made a match of it. This was embarrassing for both of us, and for a while she treated me very coldly. But we had it out together one evening in the library and decided to let the matter make no difference to us, going on as before the best of friends. I was the last person to expect a girl of eighteen to care for a man of forty, particularly one like myself, ugly and grey-haired, who had long before outworn the love of women. In fact I had to laugh, one of those sad laughs that come to us with the years, at the thought of anything so absurd; and I soon got her to give up her tragic pose and see the humour of it all as I did. So we treated it as a joke, rallied the old folks on their sentimental folly, and let it pass.

It set me thinking, however, a great deal about the girl

and her future, and I managed to make interest with several of my friends and get her invited to some good houses. Of course it was impossible to carry the old people into this galere. They were frankly impossible, but fortunately so meek and humble that it never occurred to them to assert themselves or resent their daughter going to places where they would have been refused. Uncle Gingersnaps would have paid money to stay at home, and Mrs. Grossensteck had too much homely pride to put herself in a false position. They saw indeed only another reason to be grateful to me, and another example of my surpassing kindness. Pretty, by no means a fool, and gowned by the best coutourieres of Paris, Teresa made quite a hit, and blossomed as girls do in the social sunshine. The following year, in the whirl of a gay New York winter, one would scarcely have recognised her as the same person. She had "made good," as boys say, and had used my stepping-stones to carry her far beyond my ken. In her widening interests, broader range, and increased worldly knowledge we became naturally better friends than ever and met on the common ground of those who led similar lives. What man would not value the intimacy of a young, beautiful, and clever woman? in some ways it is better than love itself, for love is a duel, with wounds given and taken, and its pleasures dearly paid for. Between Teresa and myself there was no such disturbing bond, and we were at liberty to be altogether frank in our intercourse.

One evening when I happened to be dining at the house, the absence of her father and the indisposition of her mother left us tete-a-tete in the smoking-room, whither she came to keep me company with my cigar. I saw that she was restless and with something on her mind to tell me, but I was too old a stager to force a confidence, least of all a woman's, and so I waited, said nothing, and blew smoke rings.

"Hugo," she said, "there is something I wish to speak to you about."

"I've known that for the last hour, Teresa," I said.

"This is something serious," she said, looking at me strangely.

"Blaze away," I said.

"Hugo," she broke out, "you have been borrowing money from my father."

I nodded.

"A great deal of money," she went on.

"For him - no," I said. "For me - well, yes."

"Eight or nine hundred dollars," she said.

"Those are about the figures," I returned. "Call it nine hundred."

"Oh, how could you! How could you!" she exclaimed.

I remained silent. In fact I did not know what to say.

"Don't you see the position you're putting yourself in?" she said.

"Position?" I repeated. "What position?"

"It's horrible, it's ignoble," she broke out. "I have always admired you for the way you kept yourself clear of such an ambiguous relation - you've known to the fraction of an inch what to take, what to refuse - to preserve your self-respect - my respect - unimpaired. And here I see you slipping into degradation. Oh, Hugo! I can't bear it."

"Is it such a crime to borrow a little money?" I asked.

"Not if you pay it back," she returned. "Not if you mean to pay it back. But you know you can't. You know you won't!"

"You think it's the thin edge of the wedge?" I said. "The beginning of the end and all that kind of thing?"

"You will go on," she cried. "You will become a dependent in this house, a hanger-on, a sponger. I will hate you. You will hate yourself. It went through me like a knife when I found it out."

I smoked my cigar in silence. I suppose she was quite right - horribly right, though I didn't like her any better for being so plain-spoken about it. I felt myself turning red under her gaze.

"What do you want me to do?" I said at length.

"Pay it back," she said.

"I wish to God I could," I said. "But you know how I live, Teresa, hanging on by the skin of my teeth - hardly able to keep my head above water, let alone having a dollar to spare."

"Then you can't pay," she said.

"I don't think I can," I returned.

"Then you ought to leave this house," she said.

"You have certainly made it impossible for me to stay, Teresa," I said.

"I want to make it impossible," she cried. "You - you don't understand - you think I'm cruel - it's because I like you, Hugo - it's because you're the one man I admire above anybody in the world. I'd rather see you starving than dishonoured."

"Thank you for your kind interest," I said ironically. "Under the circumstances I am almost tempted to wish you admired me less."

"Am I not right?" she demanded.

"Perfectly right," I returned. "Oh, yes! Perfectly right."

"And you'll go," she said.

"Yes, I'll go," I said.

"And earn the money and pay father?" she went on.

"And earn the money and pay father," I repeated.

"And then come back?" she added.

"Never, never, never!" I cried out.

I could see her pale under the lights.

"Oh, Hugo! don't be so ungenerous," she said. "Don't be so - so -" She hesitated, apparently unable to continue.

"Ungenerous or not," I said, "damn the words, Teresa, this isn't a time to weigh words. It isn't in flesh and blood to come back. I can't come back. Put yourself in my place."

"Some day you'll thank me," she said.

"Very possibly," I returned. "Nobody knows what may not happen. It's conceivable, of course, I might go down on my bended knees, but really, from the way I feel at this moment, I do not think it's likely."

"You want to punish me for liking you," she said.

"Teresa," I said, "I have told you already that you are right. You insist on saving me from a humiliating position. I respect your courage and your straight-forwardness. You remind me of an ancient Spartan having it out with a silly ass of a stranger who took advantage of her parents' good-nature. I am as little vain, I think, as any man, and as free from pettiness and idiotic pride - but you mustn't ask the impossible. You mustn't expect the whipped dog to come back. When I go it will be for ever."

"Then go," she said, and looked me straight in the eyes.

"I have only one thing to ask," I said. "Smooth it over to your father and mother. I am very fond of your father and mother, Teresa; I don't want them to think I've acted badly, or that I have ceased to care for them.

Tell them the necessary lies, you know."

"I will tell them," she said.

"Then good-bye," I said, rising. "I suppose I am acting like a baby to feel so sore. But I am hurt."

"Good-bye, Hugo," she said.

I went to the door and down the stairs. She followed and stood looking after me the length of the hall as I slowly put on my hat and coat. That was the last I saw of her, in the shadow of a palm, her girlish figure outlined against the black behind. I walked into the street with a heart like lead, and for the first time in my life I began to feel I was growing old.

I have been from my youth up an easy-going man, a drifter, a dawdler, always willing to put off work for play. But for once I pulled myself together, looked things in the face, and put my back to the wheel. I was determined to repay that nine hundred dollars, if I had to cut every dinner-party for the rest of the season. I was determined to repay it, if I had to work as I had never worked before. My first move was to change my address. I didn't want Uncle Gingersnaps ferreting me out, and Mrs. Grossensteck weeping on my shoulder. My next was to cancel my whole engagement book. My third, to turn over my wares and to rack my head for new ideas.

I had had a long-standing order from Granger's Weekly for a novelette. I had always hated novelettes, as one had to wait so long for one's money and then get so little; but in the humour I then found myself I plunged into the fray, if not with enthusiasm, at least with a dogged perseverance that was almost as good. Granger's Weekly liked triviality and dialogue, a lot of fuss about nothing and a happy ending. I gave it to them in a heaping measure. Dixie's Monthly, from which I had a short-story order, set dialect above rubies. I didn't know any dialect, but I borrowed a year's file and learned it like a lesson. They wrote and asked me for another on the strength of "The Courting of Amandar Jane." The Permeator was keen on Kipling and water, and I gave it to them - especially the water. Like all Southern families the Dundonalds had once had their day. I had travelled everywhere when I was a boy, and so I accordingly refreshed my dim memories with some modern travellers and wrote a short series for The Little Gentleman; "The Boy in the Carpathians," "The Boy in Old Louisiana," "A Boy in the Tyrol," "A Boy in London," "A Boy in Paris," "A Boy at the Louvre," "A Boy in Corsica," "A Boy in the Reconstruction." I reeled off about twenty of them and sold them to advantage.

It was a terribly dreary task, and I had moments of revolt when I stamped up and down my little flat and felt like throwing my resolution to the winds. But I stuck tight to the ink-bottle and fought the thing through. My novelette, strange to say, was good. Written against time and against inclination, it has always been regarded since as the best thing I ever did, and when published in book form outran three editions.

I made a thundering lot of money - for me, I mean, and in comparison to my usual income - seldom under five hundred dollars a month and often more. In eleven weeks I had repaid Grossensteck and had a credit in the bank. Nine hundred dollars has always remained to me as a unit of value, a sum of agonising significance not lightly to be spoken of, the fruits of hellish industry and self-denial. All this while I had had never a word from the Grossenstecks. At least they wrote to me often - telephoned - telegraphed - and my box at the club was choked with their letters. But I did not open a single one of them, though I found a pleasure in turning them over and over, and wondering as to what was within them. There were several in Teresa's fine hand, and these interested me most of all and tantalised me unspeakably. There was one of hers, cunningly addressed to me in a stranger's writing that I opened inadvertently; but I at once perceived the trick and had the strength of mind to throw it in the fire unread.

Perhaps you will wonder at my childishness. Sometimes I wondered at it myself. But the wound still smarted, and something stronger than I seemed to withhold me from again breaking the ice. Besides, those long lonely days, and those nights, almost as long in the retrospect, when I lay sleepless on my bed, had shown me I had been drifting into another peril no less dangerous than dependence. I had been thinking too much of the girl for my own good, and our separation had brought me to a sudden realisation of how deeply I was beginning to care for her. I hated her, too, the pitiless wretch, so there was a double reason for me not to go back.

One night as I had dressed to dine out and stepped into the street, looking up at the snow that hid the stars and silenced one's footsteps on the pavement, a woman emerged from the gloom, and before I knew what she was doing, had caught my arm. I shook her off, thinking her a beggar or something worse, and would have passed on my way had she not again struggled to detain me. I stopped, and was on the point of roughly ordering her to let me go, when I looked down into her veiled face and saw that it was Teresa Grossensteck.

"Hugo!" she said. "Hugo!"

I could only repeat her name and regard her helplessly.

"Hugo," she said, "I am cold. Take me upstairs. I am chilled through and through."

"Oh, but Teresa," I expostulated, "it wouldn't be right. You know it wouldn't be right. You might be seen."

She laid her hand, her ungloved, icy hand, against my cheek.

"I have been here an hour," she said. "Take me to your rooms. I am freezing."

I led her up the stairs and to my little apartment. I seated her before the fire, turned up the lights, and stood and looked at her.

"What have you come here for?" I said. "I've paid your father - paid him a month ago."

She made no answer, but spread her hands before the fire and shivered in the glow. She kept her eyes fixed on the coals in front of her and put out the tips of her little slippered feet. Then I perceived that she was in a ball gown and that her arms were bare under her opera cloak.

At last she broke the silence.

"How cheerless your room is," she said, looking about.

Lloyd Osbourne

"Oh, how cheerless!"

"Did you come here to tell me that?" I said.

"No," she said. "I don't know why I came. Because I was a fool, I suppose - a fool to think you'd want to see me. Take me home, Hugo." She rose as she said this and looked towards the door. I pressed her to take a little whiskey, for she was still as cold as death and as white as the snow queen in Hans Andersen's tale, but she refused to let me give her any.

"Take me home, please," she repeated.

Her carriage was waiting a block away. Hendricks, the footman, received my order with impassivity and shut us in together with the unconcern of a good servant. It was dark in the carriage, and neither of us spoke as we whirled through the snowy streets. Once the lights of a passing hansom illumined my companion's face and I saw that she was crying. It pleased me to see her suffer; she had cost me eleven weeks of misery; why should she escape scot-free!

"Hugo," she said, "are you coming back to us, Hugo?"

"I don't know," I said.

"Why don't you know?" she asked.

"Oh, because!" I said.

"That's no answer," she said.

There was a pause.

"I was beginning to care too much about you," I said. "I think I was beginning to fall in love with you. I've got out of one false position. Why should I blunder into another?"

"Would it be a false position to love me?" she said.

"Of course that would a good deal depend on you," I said.

"Suppose I wanted you to," she said.

"Oh, but you couldn't!" I said.

"Why couldn't I?" she said.

"But forty," I objected; "nobody loves anybody who's forty, you know."

"I do," she said, "though, come to think of it, you were thirty-nine - when - when it first happened, Hugo."

I put out my arms in the dark and caught her to me. I could not believe my own good fortune as I felt her trembling and crying against my breast. I was humbled and ashamed. It was like a dream. An old fellow like me - forty, you know.

"It was a mighty near thing, Teresa," I said.

"I guess it was - for me!" she said.

"I meant myself, sweetheart," I said.

"For both of us then," she said, in a voice between

laughter and tears, and impulsively put her arms round my neck.

THE AWAKENING OF GEORGE RAYMOND

I

George Raymond's father had been a rich man, rich in those days before the word millionaire had been invented, and when a modest hundred thousand, lent out at an interest varying from ten to fifteen per cent, brought in an income that placed its possessor on the lower steps of affluence. He was the banker of a small New Jersey town, a man of portentous respectability, who proffered two fingers to his poorer clients and spoke about the weather as though it belonged to him. When the school-children read of Croesus in their mythology, it was Jacob Raymond they saw in their mind's eye; such expressions as "rich beyond the dreams of avarice" suggested him as inevitably as pumpkin did pie; they wondered doubtfully about him in church when that unfortunate matter of the camel was brought up with its attendant difficulties for the wealthy. Even Captain Kidd's treasure, in those times so actively sought for along the whole stretch of the New England coast, conjured up a small brick building with "Jacob Raymond, Banker" in gilt letters above the lintel of the door.

But there came a day when that door stayed locked and a hundred white faces gathered about it, blocking the village street and talking in whispers though the noonday sun was shining. Raymond's bank was insolvent, and the banker himself, a fugitive in tarry sea clothes, was hauling ropes on a vessel outward bound for Callao. He might have stayed in Middleborough and braved it out, for he had robbed no man and his personal honour was untarnished, having succumbed without dishonesty to primitive methods and lack of capital. But he chose instead the meaner course of flight. Of all the reproachful faces he left behind him his wife's was the one he felt himself the least able to confront; and thus, abandoning everything, with hardly a dozen dollars in his pocket, he slipped away to sea, never to be seen or heard of again.

Mrs. Raymond was a woman of forty-five, a New Englander to her finger-tips, proud, arrogant, and fiercely honest; a woman who never forgot, never forgave, and who practised her narrow Christianity with the unrelentingness of an Indian. She lived up to an austere standard herself, and woe betide those who fell one whit behind her. She was one of those just persons who would have cast the first stone at the dictates of conscience and with a sort of holy joy in her own fitness to do so. For years she had been the richest woman in Middleborough, the head of everything charitable and religious, the mainstay of ministers, the court of final appeal in the case of sinners and backsliders. Now, in a moment, through no fault of her own, the whole fabric of her life had crumbled. Again had the mighty fallen.

She had not a spark of pity for her husband. To owe what you could not pay was to her the height of dishonour. It was theft, and she had no compunction in giving it the name, however it might be disguised or palliated. She could see no mitigating circumstances in Raymond's disgrace, and the fact that she was innocently involved in his downfall filled her with exasperation. The big old corner house was her own. She had been born in it. It had been her marriage portion from her father. She put it straightway under the hammer; her canal stock with it; her furniture and linen; a row of five little cottages on the outskirts of the town where five poor families had found not only that their bodies, but the welfare of their souls, had been confided to her grim keeping. She stripped herself of everything, and when all had been made over to the creditors there still remained a deficit of seventeen hundred dollars. This debt which was not a debt, for she was under no legal compulsion to pay a penny of it, would willingly have been condoned by men already grateful for her generosity; but she would hear of no such compromise, not even that her notes be free of interest, and she gave them at five per cent, resolute that in time she would redeem them to the uttermost farthing.

Under these sudden changes of fortune it is seldom that the sufferer remains amid the ruins of past prosperity. The human instinct is to fly and hide. The wound heals more readily amongst strangers. The material evils of life are never so intolerable as the public loss of caste. It may be said that it is people, not things, which cause most of the world's unhappiness. Mrs. Raymond came to New York, where she had not a friend except the son she brought with her, there to set herself with an undaunted heart to earn the seventeen hundred dollars she had voluntarily taken on her shoulders to repay.

George Raymond, her son, was then a boy of fifteen. High-strung, high-spirited, with all the seriousness of a youngster who had prematurely learned to think for himself, he had arrived at the age when ineffaceable impressions are made and the tendencies of a lifetime decided. Passionately attached to his father, he had lost him in a way that would have made death seem preferable. He saw his mother, so shortly before the great lady of a little town, working out like a servant in other people's houses. The tragedy of it all ate into his soul and overcame him with a sense of hopelessness and despair. It would not have been so hard could he have helped, even in a small way, towards the recovery of their fortunes; but his mother, faithful even in direst poverty to her New England blood, sent him to school, determined that at any sacrifice he should finish his education. But by degrees Mrs. Raymond drifted into another class of work. She became a nurse, and, in a situation where her conscientiousness was invaluable, slowly established a connection that in time kept her constantly busy. She won the regard of an important physician, and not only won it but kept it, and thus little by little found her way into good houses, where she was highly paid and treated with consideration.

Had it not been for the seventeen hundred dollars and the five per cent interest upon it, she could have earned enough to keep herself and her son very comfortable in the three rooms they occupied on Seventh Street. But this debt, ever present in the minds of both mother and son, hung over them like a cloud and took every penny there was to spare. Those two years from fifteen to seventeen were the most terrible in Raymond's life. At an age when he possessed neither philosophy nor knowledge and yet the fullest capacity to suffer, he had to bear, with what courage he could muster, the crudest buffets of an adverse fate.

Raymond drudged at his books, passed from class to class and returned at night to the empty rooms he called home, where he cooked his own meals and sat solitary beside the candle until it was the hour for bed. His mother was seldom there to greet him. As a nurse she was kept prisoner, for weeks at a time, in the houses where she was engaged. It meant much to the boy to find a note from her lying on the table when he returned at night; more still to wait at street corners in his shabby overcoat for those appointments she often made with him. When she took infectious cases and dared neither write nor speak to him, they had an hour planned beforehand when she would smile at him from an open window and wave her hand.

But she was not invariably busy. There were intervals between her engagements when she remained at home; when those rooms, ordinarily so lonely and still, took on a wonderful brightness with her presence; when Raymond, coming back from school late in the after-noon, ran along the streets singing, as he thought of his mother awaiting him. This stern woman, the harsh daughter of a harsh race, had but a single streak of tenderness in her withered heart. To her son she gave transcendent love, and the whole of her starved nature went out to him in immeasurable devotion. Their poverty, the absence of all friends, the burden of debt, the unacknowledged disgrace, and (harder still to bear) the long and enforced separations from each other, all served to draw the pair into the closest intimacy. Raymond grew towards manhood without ever having met a girl of his own age; without ever having had a chum; without knowing the least thing of youth save much of its green-sickness and longing.

When the great debt had been paid off and the last of

Lloyd Osbourne

the notes cancelled there came no corresponding alleviation of their straitened circumstances. Raymond had graduated from the High School and was taking the medical course at Columbia University. Every penny was put by for the unavoidable expenses of his tuition. The mother, shrewd, ambitious, and far-seeing, was staking everything against the future, and was wise enough to sacrifice the present in order to launch her son into a profession. In those days fresh air had not been discovered. Athletics, then in their infancy, were regarded much as we now do prize-fighting. The ideal student was a pale individual who wore out the night with cold towels around his head, and who had a bigger appetite for books than for meat. Docile, unquestioning, knowing no law but his mother's wish; eager to earn her commendation and to repay with usury the immense sacrifices she had made for him, Raymond worked himself to a shadow with study, and at nineteen was a tall, thin, narrow-shouldered young man with sunken cheeks and a preternatural whiteness of complexion.

He was far from being a bad-looking fellow, however. He had beautiful blue eyes, more like a girl's than a man's, and there was something earnest and winning in his face that often got him a shy glance on the street from passing women. His acquaintance in this direction went no further. Many times when a college acquaintance would have included him in some little party, his mother had peremptorily refused to let him go. Her face would darken with jealousy and anger, nor was she backward with a string of reasons for her refusal. It would unsettle him; he had no money to waste on girls; he would be shamed by his shabby clothes and ungloved hands; they would laugh at him behind his back; was he tired, then, of his old mother who had worked so hard to bring him up decently? And so on and so on, until, without knowing exactly why, Raymond would feel himself terribly in the wrong, and was glad enough at last to be forgiven on the understanding that he would never propose such a reprehensible thing again.

In any other young man, brought up in the ordinary way, with the ordinary advantages, such submission would have seemed mean-spirited; but the bond between these two was riveted with memories of penury and privation; any appeal to those black days brought Raymond on his knees; it was intolerable to him that he should ever cause a pang in his dear mother's breast. Thus, at the age when the heart is hungriest for companionship; when for the first time a young man seems to discover the existence of a hitherto unknown and unimportant sex; when an inner voice urges him to take his place in the ranks and keep step with the mighty army of his generation, Raymond was doomed to walk alone, a wistful outcast, regarding his enviable companions from afar.

He was in his second year at college when his studies were broken off by his mother's illness. He was suddenly called home to find her delirious in bed, struck down in the full tide of strength by the disease she had taken from a patient. It was scarlet fever, and when it had run its course the doctor took him to one side and told him that his mother's nursing days were over. During her tedious convalescence, as Raymond would sit beside her bed and read aloud to her, their eyes were constantly meeting in unspoken appre-hension. They saw the ground, so solid a month before, now crumbling beneath their feet; their struggles, their makeshifts, their starved and meagre life had all been in vain. Their little savings were gone; the bread-winner, tempting fate once too often, had received what was to her worse than a mortal wound, for the means of livelihood had been taken from her.

"Could I have but died," she repeated to herself. "Oh, could I have but died!"

Raymond laid his head against the coverlet and sobbed. He needed no words to tell him what was in her mind; that her illness had used up the little money there was to spare; that she, so long the support of both, was now a helpless burden on his hands. Pity for her outweighed every other consideration. His own loss seemed but little in comparison to hers. It was the concluding tragedy of those five tragic years. The battle, through no fault of theirs, had gone against them. The dream of a professional career was over.

His mother grew better. The doctor ceased his visits. She was able to get on her feet again. She took over their pinched housekeeping. But her step was heavy; the gaunt, grim straight-backed woman, with her thin grey hair and set mouth, was no more than a spectre of her former self. The doctor was right. There was nothing before her but lifelong invalidism.

Raymond found work; a place in the auditing department of a railroad, with a salary to begin with of sixty dollars a month; in ten years he might hope to get a hundred. But he was one of those whose back bent easily to misfortune. Heaven knew, he had been schooled long enough to take its blows with fortitude. His mother and he could manage comfortably on sixty dollars a month; and when he laid his first earnings in her hand he even smiled with satisfaction. She took the money in silence, her heart too full to ask him whence it came. She had hoped against hope until that moment; and the bills, as she looked at them, seemed to sting her shrivelled hand.

One day, as she was cleaning her son's room, she opened a box that stood in the corner, and was surprised to find it contain a package done up in wrapping paper. She opened it with curiosity and the tears sprang to her eyes as she saw the second-hand medical books George had used at college. Here they were, in neat wrappers, laid by for ever. Too precious to throw away, too articulate of unfulfilled ambitions to stand exposed on shelves, they had been laid away in the grave of her son's hopes. She did them up again with trembling fingers, and that night when George returned to supper, he found his mother in the dark, crying.

II

In the years from nineteen to forty-two most men have fulfilled their destiny; those who have had within them the ability to rise have risen; the weak, the wastrels, the mediocrities have shaken down into their appointed places. Even the bummer has his own particular bit of wall in front of the saloon and his own particular chair within. Those who have something to do are busy doing it, whatever it may be. In the human comedy everyone in time finds his role and must play it to the end, happy indeed if he be cast in a part that at all suits him.

George Raymond at forty-two was still in the auditor's department of the New York Central. Time had wrinkled his cheek, had turned his brown hair to a crisp grey, had bowed his shoulders to the desk he had used for twenty-two years. His eyes alone retained their boyish brightness, and a sort of appealing look as of one who his whole life long had been a dependent on other people. As an automaton, a mere cog in a vast machine, he had won the praise of his superiors by his complete self-effacement. He was never ill, never absent, never had trouble with his subordinates, never talked back, never made complaints, and, in the flattering language of the superintendent, "he knew what he knew!"

In the office, as in every other aggregation of human beings, there were coteries, cliques, friendships and hatreds, jealousies, heart-burnings and vendettas. There was scarcely a man there without friends or foes. Raymond alone had neither. To the others he was a strange, silent, unknown creature whose very address was a matter of conjecture; a man who did not drink, did not smoke, did not talk; who ate four bananas for his lunch and invariably carried a book in the pocket of his shabby coat. It was said of him that once, during a terrible blizzard, he had been the only clerk to reach the office; that he had worked there stark alone until one o'clock, when at the stroke of the hour he had taken out his four bananas and his book! There were other stories about him of the same kind, not all of them true to fate, but essentially true of the man's nature and of his rigid adherence to routine. He had risen, place by place, to a position that gave him a hundred and fifty dollars a month, and one so responsible that his death or absence would have dislocated the office for half a day.

"A first-class man and an authority on pro ratas!"

Such might have been the inscription on George Raymond's tomb!

His mother was still alive. She had never entirely regained her health or her strength, and it took all the little she had of either to do the necessary house-keeping for herself and her son. Thin to emaciation, sharp-tongued, a tyrant to her finger-tips, her indomi-table spirit remained as uncowed as ever and she ruled her son with a rod of iron. To her, Georgie, as she always called him, was still a child. As far as she was concerned he had never grown up. She took his month's salary, told him when to buy new shirts, ordered his clothes herself, doled out warningly the few dollars for his necessaries, and saved, saved, continually saved. The old woman dreaded poverty with a horror not to be expressed in words. It had ruined her own life; it had crushed her son under its merciless wheels; in the words of the proverb, she was the coward who died a thousand deaths in the agonies of apprehension. She was one of those not uncommon misers, who hoard, not for love of money, but through fear. She had managed, with penurious thrift and a self-denial almost sublime in its austerity, to set a side eight thousand dollars. Eight thousand dollars from an income that began at sixty and rose to a little under three times that amount! Eight thousand dollars, wrung from their lives at the price of every joy, every alleviation, everything that could make the world barely tolerable.

Every summer Raymond had a two-weeks' holiday, which he spent at Middleborough with some relatives of his father's. He had the pronounced love of the sea that is usual with those born and bred in seaport towns. His earliest memories went back to great deep-water ships, their jib-booms poking into the second-story windows of the city front, their decks hoarsely melodious with the yo-heave-yo of straining seamen. The smell of tar, the sight of enormous anchors impending above the narrow street, the lofty masts piercing the sky in a tangle of ropes and blocks, the exotic cargoes mountains high - all moved him like a poem. He knew no pleasure like that of sailing his cousin's sloop; he loved every plank of her dainty hull; it was to him a privilege to lay his hand to any task appertaining to her, however humble or hard. To calk, to paint, to polish brasswork; to pump out bilge; to set up the rigging; to sit cross-legged and patch sails; and, best of all, to put her lee rail under in a spanking breeze and race her seaward against the mimic fleet - Ah, how swiftly those bright days passed, how bitter was the parting and the return, all too soon, to the dingy offices of the railroad.

It never occurred to him to think his own lot hard, or to contrast himself with other men of his age, who at forty-two were mostly substantial members of society, with interests, obligations, responsibilities, to which he himself was an utter stranger. Under the iron bondage of his mother he had remained a child. To displease her seemed the worst thing that could befall him; to win her commendation filled him with content. But there were times, guiltily remembered and put by with shame, when he longed for something more from life; when the sight of a beautiful woman on the street reminded him of his own loneliness and isolation; when he was overcome with a sudden surging sense that he was an outsider in the midst of these teeming thousands, unloved and old, without friends or hope or future to look forward to. He would reproach himself for such lawless repining, for such disloyalty to his mother. Was not her case worse than his? Did she not lecture him on the duty of cheerfulness, she the invalid, racked with pains, with nerves, who practised so pitifully what she preached? The tears would come to his eyes. No, he would not ask the impossible; he would go his way, brave and uncomplaining, and let the empty years roll over his head without a murmur against fate.

But the years, apparently so void, were screening a strange and undreamed-of part for him to play. The Spaniards, a vague, almost legendary people, as remote from Raymond's life as the Assamese or the cliff-dwellers of New Mexico, began to take on a concrete character, and were suddenly discovered to be the enemies of the human race. Raymond grew accusto-med to the sight of Cuban flags, at first so unfamiliar, and then, later, so touching in their significance. Newspaper pictures of Gomez and Garcia were tacked on the homely walls of barber-shops, in railroad shops, in grubby offices and cargo elevators, and with them savage caricatures of a person called Weyler, and referring bitterly to other persons (who seemed in a bad way) called the reconcentrados. Raymond wondered what it was all about; bought books to elucidate the matter; took fire with indignation and resentment. Then came the Maine affair; the suspense of seventy million people eager to avenge their dead; the decision of the court of inquiry; the emergency vote; the preparation for war. Raymond watched it all with a curious detachment. He never realised that it could have anything personally to do with him. The long days in the auditor's department went on undisturbed for all that the country was arming and the State governors were calling out their quotas of men. Two of his associates quitted their desks and changed their black coats for army blue. Raymond admired them; envied them; but it never occurred to him to ask why they should go and he should stay. It was natural for him to stay; it was inevitable; he was as much a part of the office as the office floor.

One afternoon, going home on the Elevated, he overheard two men talking.

"I don't know what we'll do," said one.

"Oh, there are lots of men," said the other.

"Men, yes - but no sailors," said the first.

"That's right," said the other.

"We are at our wits' end to man the new ships," said the first.

"What did you total up to-day?" said the other.

His companion shrugged his shoulders.

"Eighty applicants, and seven taken," he said.

"And those foreigners?"

"All but two!"

"There's danger in that kind of thing!"

"Yes, indeed, but what can you do?"

The words rang in Raymond's head. That night he hardly slept. He was in the throes of making a tremendous resolution, he who, for forty years, had been tied to his mother's apron string. Making it of his own volition, unprompted, at the behest of no one save, perhaps, the man in the car, asserting at last his manhood in defiance of the subjection that had never come home to him until that moment. He rose in the morning, pale and determined. He felt a hypocrite through and through as his mother commented on his looks and grew anxious as he pushed away his untasted breakfast. It came over him afresh how good she was, how tender. He did not love her less because his great purpose had been taken. He knew how she would suffer, and the thought of it racked his heart; he was tempted to take her into his confidence, but dared not, distrusting his own powers of resistance were she to say no. So he kissed her instead, with greater warmth than usual, and left the house with misty eyes. He got an extension of the noon hour and hurried down to the naval recruiting office. It was doing a brisk business in turning away applicants, and from the bottom of the line Raymond was not kept waiting long before he attained the top; and from thence in his turn was led into an inner office. He was briefly examined as to his sea experience. Could he box the compass? He could. Could he make a long splice? He could. What was meant by the monkey-gaff of a full-rigged ship? He told them. What was his reason in wanting to join the Navy? Because he thought he'd like to do something for his country. Very good; turn him over to the doctor; next! Then the doctor weighed him, looked at his teeth, hit him in the chest, listened to his heart, thumped and questioned him, and then passed him on to a third person to be enrolled.

When George Raymond emerged into the open air it was as a full A B in the service of the United States

This announcement at the office made an extraordinary sensation. Men he hardly knew shook hands with him and clapped him on the back. He was taken upstairs to be impressively informed that his position would be held open for him. On every side he saw kindling faces, smiling glances of approbation, the quick passing of the news in whispers. He had suddenly risen from obscurity to become part of the War; the heir of a wonderful and possibly tragic future; a patriot; a hero! It was a bewildering experience and not without its charm. He was surprised to find himself still the same man.

The scene at home was less enthusiastic. It was even mortifying, and Georgie, as his mother invariably called him, had to endure a storm of sarcasm and reproaches. The old woman's ardent patriotism stopped short at giving up her son. It was the duty of others to fight, Georgie's to stay at home with his mother. He let her talk herself out, saying little, but regarding her with a grave, kind obstinacy. Then she broke down, weeping and clinging to him. Somehow, though he could hardly explain it to himself, the relation between the two underwent a change. He left that house the unquestioned master of himself, the acknowledged head of that tiny household; he had won, and his victory instead of abating by a hair's-breadth his mother's love for him had drawn the pair closer to each other than ever before. Though she had no articulate conception of it Georgie had risen enormously in his mother's respect. The woman had given way to the man, and the eternal fitness of things had been vindicated.

Her tenderness and devotion were redoubled. Never had there been such a son in the history of the world. She relaxed her economies in order to buy him little delicacies, such as sardines and pickles; and when soon after his enlistment his uniform came home she spread it on her bed and cried, and then sank on her knees, passionately kissing the coarse serge. In the limitation of her horizon she could see but a single figure. It was Georgie's country, Georgie's President, Georgie's fleet, Georgie's righteous quarrel in the cause of stifled freedom. To her, it was Georgie's war with Spain.

He was drafted aboard the Dixie, where, within a week of his joining, he was promoted to be one of the four quartermasters. So much older than the majority of his comrades, quick, alert, obedient, and responsible, he was naturally amongst the first chosen for what are called leading seamen. Never was a man more in his element than George Raymond. He shook down into naval life like one born to it. The sea was in his blood, and his translation from the auditor's department to the deck of a fighting ship seemed to him like one of those happy dreams when one pinches himself to try and confirm the impossible. Metaphorically speaking, he was always pinching himself and contrasting the monotonous past with the glorious and animated present. The change told in his manner, in the tilt of his head, in his fearless eyes and straighter back. It comes natural to heroes to protrude their chests and walk upon air; and it is pardonable, indeed, in war time, when each feels himself responsible for a fraction of his country's honour.

"Georgie, you are positively becoming handsome," said his mother.

Amongst Raymond's comrades on the Dixie was a youngster of twenty-one, named Howard Quintan. Something attracted him in the boy, and he went out of his way to make things smooth for him aboard. The liking was no less cordially returned, and the two became fast friends. One day, when they were both given liberty together, Howard insisted on taking him to his own home.

"The folks want to know you," he said. "They naturally think a heap of you because I do, and I've told them how good you've been and all that."

"Oh, rubbish!" said Raymond, though he was inwardly pleased. At the time they were walking up Fifth Avenue, both in uniform, with their caps on one side, sailor fashion, and their wide trousers flapping about their ankles. People looked at them kindly as they passed, for the shadow of the war lay on everyone and all hearts went out to the men who were to uphold the flag. Raymond was flattered and yet somewhat overcome by the attention his companion and he excited.

"Let's get out of this, Quint," he said. "I can't walk straight when people look at me like that. Don't you feel kind of givey-givey at the knees with all those pretty girls loving us in advance?"

"Oh, that's what I like!" said Quintan. "I never got a glance when I used to sport a silk hat. Besides, here we are at the old stand!"

Raymond regarded him with blank surprise as they turned aside and up the steps of one of the houses.

"Land's sake!" he exclaimed; "you don't mean to say you live in a place like this? Here?" he added, with an intonation that caused Howard to burst out laughing.

The young fellow pushed by the footman that admitted them and ran up the stairs three steps at a time. Raymond followed more slowly, dazed by the splendour he saw about him, and feeling horribly embarrassed and deserted. He halted on the stairs as he saw Quintan throw his arms about a tall, stately, magnificently dressed woman and kiss her boisterously; and he was in two minds whether or not to slink down again and disappear, when his companion called out to him to hurry up.

"Mother, this is Mr. Raymond," he said. "He's the best friend I have on the Dixie, and you're to be awfully good to him!"

Mrs. Quintan graciously gave him her hand and said something about his kindness to her boy. Raymond was too stricken to speak and was thankful for the semi-darkness that hid his face. Mrs. Quintan continued softly, in the same sweet and overpowering manner, to purr her gratitude and try to put him at his ease. Raymond would have been a happy man could he have sunk though the parquetry floor. He trembled as he was led into the drawing-room, where another gracious and overpowering creature rose to receive them.

"My aunt, Miss Christine Latimer," said Howard.

She was younger than Mrs. Quintan; a tall, fair woman of middle age, with a fine figure, hair streaked with grey, and the remains of what had once been extreme beauty. Her voice was the sweetest Raymond had ever listened to, and his shyness and agitation wore off as she began to speak to him. He was left a long while alone with her, for Howard and his mother withdrew, excusing themselves on the score of private matters. Christine Latimer was touched by the forlorn quarter-master, who, in his nervousness, gripped his chair with clenched hands and started when he was asked a question. She soon got him past this stage of their acquaintance, and, leading him on by gentle gradations to talk about himself, even learned his whole story, and that in so unobtrusive a fashion that he was hardly aware of his having told it to her.

"I am speaking to you as though I had known you all my life," he said in an artless compliment. "I hope it is not very forward of me. It is your fault for being so kind and good."

He was ecstatic when he left the house with Quintan.

"I didn't know there were such women in the world," he said. "So noble, so winning and high-bred. It makes you understand history to meet people like that. Mary Queen of Scots, Marie Antoinette and all those, you know - they must have been like that. I - I could understand a man dying for Miss Latimer!"

"Oh, she's all right, my aunt!" said Quintan. "She was a tremendous beauty once, and even now she's what I'd call a devilish handsome woman. And the grand manner, it isn't everybody that likes it, but I do. It's a little old-fashioned nowadays, but, by Jove, it still tells."

"I wonder that such a splendid woman should have remained unmarried," said Raymond. He stuck an instant on the word unmarried. It seemed almost common to apply to such a princess.

"She had an early love affair that turned out badly," said Quintan. "I don't know what went wrong, but anyway it didn't work. Then, when my father died, she came to live with us and help bring us up - you see there are two more of us in the family - and I am told she refused some good matches just on account of us kids. It makes me feel guilty sometimes to think of it."

"Why guilty?" asked Raymond.

"Because none of us were worth it, old chap," said Quintan.

"I'm sure she never thought so," observed Raymond.

"My aunt's rather an unusual woman," said Quintan. "She has voluntarily played second fiddle all her life; and, between you and me, you know, my mother's a bit of a tyrant, and not always easy to get along with - so it wasn't so simple a game as it looks."

Raymond was shocked at this way of putting the matter.

"You mean she sacrificed the best years of her life for you," he said stiffly.

"Women are like that - good women," said Quintan. "Catch a man being such a fool - looking at it generally, you know - me apart. She had a tidy little fortune from her father, and might have had a yard of her own to play in, but our little baby hands held her tight."

Raymond regarded his companion's hands. They were large and red, and rough with the hard work on board the Dixie; regarded them respectfully, almost with awe, for had they not restrained that glorious being in the full tide of her youth and beauty!

"Now it's too late," said Quintan.

"What do you mean by too late?" asked the quartermaster.

"Well, she's passed forty," said Quintan. "The babies have grown up, and the selfish beasts are striking out for themselves. Her occupation's gone, and she's left plante la. Worse than that, my mother, who never bothered two cents about us then, now loves us to distraction. And, when all's said, you know, it's natural to like your mother best!"

"Too bad!" ejaculated Raymond.

"I call it deuced hard luck," said Quintan. "My mother really neglected us shamefully, and it was Aunt Christine who brought us up and blew our noses and rubbed us with goose-grease when we had croup, and all that kind of thing. Then, when we grew up, my mother suddenly discovered her long-lost children and began to think a heap of us - after having scamped the whole business for fifteen years - and my aunt, who was the real nigger in the hedge, got kind of let out, you see."

Raymond did not see, and he was indignant, besides, at the coarseness of his companion's expressions. So he walked along and said nothing.

"And, as I said before, it's now too late," said Quintan.

"Too late for what?" demanded Raymond, who was deeply interested.

"For her to take up with anybody else," said Quintan. "To marry, you know. She sacrificed all her opportunities for us; and now, in the inevitable course of things, we are kind of abandoning her when she is old and faded and lonely."

"I consider your aunt one of the most beautiful women in the world," protested Raymond.

"But you can't put back the clock, old fellow," said Quintan. "What has the world to offer to an old maid of forty-two? There she is in the empty nest, and not her own nest at that, with all her little nestlings flying over the hills and far away, and the genuine mother-bird varying the monotony by occasionally pecking her eyes out."

Raymond did not know what to answer. He could not be so rude as to make any reflection on Mrs. Quintan, though he was stirred with resentment against her. This noble, angelic, saintly woman, who in every gesture reminded him of dead queens and historic personages! It went to his heart to think of her, bereft and lonely, in that splendid house he had so lately quitted. He recognised, in the unmistakable accord between him and her, the fellowship of a pair who, in different ways and in different stations, had yet fought and suffered and endured for what they judged their duty. Forty-two years old! Singular coincidence, in itself almost a bond between them, that he, too, was of an identical age. Forty-two! Why, it was called the prime of life. He inhaled a deep breath of air; it was the prime of life; until then no one had really begun to live!

"Why don't you say something?" said Quintan.

"I was just thinking how mistaken you were," returned Raymond. "There must be hundreds of men who would be proud to win her slightest regard; who, instead of considering her faded or old, would choose her out of a thousand of younger women and would be happy for ever if she would take - " He was going to say them, but that sounded improper, and he changed it, at the cost of grammar, to "him."

Quintan laughed at his companion's vehemence, and the subject passed and gave way to another about shrapnel. But he did not fail, later on, to carry a humorous report of the conversation to his aunt.

"What have you been doing to my old quartermaster?" he said. "Hasn't the poor fellow enough troubles as it is, without falling in love with you! He can't talk of anything else, and blushes like a girl when he mentions your name. He told me yesterday he was willing to die for a woman like you."

"I think he's a dear, nice fellow," said Miss Latimer, "and if he wants to love me he can. It will keep him out of mischief!"

Raymond saw a great deal of Miss Latimer in the month before they sailed south. Quintan took him constantly to the house, where, in his capacity of humble and devoted comrade, the tall quartermaster was always welcome and made much of. Mrs. Quintan was alive to the value of this attached follower, who might be trusted to guard her son in the perils that lay before him. She treated him as a sort of combination of valet, nurse, and poor relation, asking him all sorts of intimate questions about Howard's socks and under-clothing, and holding him altogether responsible for the boy's welfare. Her tone was one of anxious patronage, touching at times on a deeper emotion when she often broke down and cried. The quartermaster was greatly moved by her trust in him. The tears would come to his own eyes, and he would try in his clumsy way to comfort her, promising that, so far as it lay with him, Howard should return safe and sound. In his self-abnegation it never occurred to him that his own life was as valuable as Howard Quintan's. He acquiesced in the understanding that it was his business to get Howard through the war unscratched, at whatever risk or jeopardy to himself.

Those were wonderful days for him. To be an intimate of that splendid household, to drive behind spanking bays with Miss Latimer by his side, to take tea at the Waldorf with her and other semi-divine beings - what a dazzling experience for the ex-clerk, whose lines so recently had lain in such different places. Innately a gentleman, he bore himself with dignity in this new position, with a fine simplicity and self-effacement that was not lost on some of his friends. His respect for them all was unbounded. For the mother, so majestic, so awe-inspiring; for Howard, that handsome boy whose exuberant Americanism was untouched by any feeling of caste; for Melton and Hubert Henry, his brothers, those lordly striplings of a lordly race; for Miss Latimer, who in his heart of hearts he dared not call Christine, and who to him was the embodiment of everything adorable in women. Yes, he loved her; confessed to himself that he loved her; humbly and without hope, with no anticipation of anything more between them, overcome indeed that his presumption should go thus far.

He did not attempt to hide his feelings for her, and though too shy for any expression of it, and withheld besides by the utter impossibility of such a suit, he betrayed himself to her in a thousand artless ways. He asked for no higher happiness than to sit by her side, looking into her face and listening to her mellow voice. He was thrice happy were he privileged to touch her hand in passing a teacup. Her gentleness and courtesy, her evident consideration, the little peeps she gave him into a nature gracious and refined beyond anything he had ever known, all transported him with unreasoning delight. She, on her part, so accustomed to play a minor role herself in her sister's household, was yet too much a woman not to like an admirer of her own. She took more pains with her dress, looked at herself more often in the glass than she had done in years. It was laughable; it was absurd; and she joined as readily as anyone in the mirth that Raymond's devotion excited in the family, but, deep down within her, she was pleased. At the least it showed she had not grown too old to make men love her; it was the vindication of the mounting years; the time, then, had not yet come when she had ceased altogether to count. She had lost her nephews, who were growing to be men; the love she put by so readily when it was in her reach seemed now more precious as she beheld her faded and diminished beauty, the crow's-feet about her eyes, her hair turning from brown to grey. A smothered voice within her said: "Why not?"

She analysed Raymond narrowly in the long tete-a-tetes they had together. She drew him out, encouraging and pressing him to tell her everything about himself. She was always apprehending a jarring note, the inevitable sign of the man's coarser clay, of his comm.-oner upbringing, the clash of his caste on hers. But she was struck instead by his inherent refinement, by his unformulated instincts of well-doing and honour. He was hazy about the use of oyster-forks, had never seen a finger-bowl, committed to her eyes a dozen little solecisms which he hastened to correct by frankly asking her assistance; but in the true essentials she never had to feel any shame for him. Clumsy, grotesquely ignorant of the social amenities, he was yet a gentleman.

The night before they were to sail, he came to say good-bye. The war had at last begun in earnest; men were falling, and the Spaniards were expected to make a desperate and bloody resistance. It was a sobering moment for everyone, and, in all voices, however hard they tried to make them brave and gay, there ran an undercurrent of solemnity. Howard and Raymond were to be actors in that terrible drama not yet played; stripped and powder-blackened at their guns, they were perhaps doomed to go down with their ship and find their graves in the Caribbean. Before them lay untold possibilities of wounds and mutilation, of disease, suffering, and horror. What woman that knew them could look on unmoved at the sight of these men, so grave and earnest, so quietly resolute, so deprecatory of anything like braggadocio or over-confidence? It filled Christine Latimer with a fierce pride in herself and them; in a race that could breed men so gentle and so brave; in a country that was founded so surely on the devoted hearts of its citizens.

She was crying as Raymond came to her later on the same evening, and found her sitting in the far end of the drawing-room with the lights turned low. They were alone together, for the quartermaster had left Howard with his mother and his brothers gathered in a farewell group about the library fire. Miss Latimer took both of Raymond's hands, and, with no attempt to disguise her sorrow, drew him close beside her on the divan. She was overflowing with pity for this poor fellow, whose life had been so hard, in which until now there had neither been love nor friends, whose only human tie was to his mother and to her. Had he known it, he might have put his arms about her and kissed her tear-swollen eyes and drawn her head against his breast. She was filled with a pent-up tenderness for him; a word, and she would have discovered what was until then inarticulate in her bosom. But the tall quartermaster was withheld from such incredible presumption. Her beautiful gown against his common serge typified, as it were, the gulf between them. Her distress, her agitation, were in his mind due to her concern for Howard Quintan; and he told her again and again, with manly sincerity, that he would take good care of her boy.

She knew he loved her. It had been plain to her for weeks past. She knew every thought in his head as he sat there beside her, thrilled with the touch of her hands, and in the throes of a respectful rapture. Again and again the avowal was on his lips; he longed to tell her how dear she was to him; it would be hard to die with that unsaid, were he to be amongst those who never returned. It never occurred to him that she might return his love. A woman like her! A queen!

She could easily have helped him out. More than once she was on the point of doing so. But the woman in her rebelled at the thought of taking what was the man's place. She had something of the exaggerated delicacy of an old maid. It was for him to ask, for her to answer; and the precious moments slipped away. At last, greatly daring, he managed to blurt out the fact that he wanted to ask a favour.

"A favour?" she said.

"Won't you give me something," he said timidly, "some little thing to take with me to remember you by?"

She replied she would with pleasure. She wanted him to remember her. What was it that he would like?

"There is nothing I could refuse you," she said, smiling.

Raymond was overcome with embarrassment. She saw him looking at her hair; her hair which was her greatest beauty, and which when undone was luxuriant enough to reach below her waist. He had often expressed his admiration for it.

"What would you like?" she asked again.

"Oh, anything," he faltered. "A - a book!"

She could not restrain her laughter. A book! She laughed and laughed. She seemed carried away by an extraordinary merriment. Raymond thought he had never heard a woman laugh like that before. It made him feel very badly. He wondered what it was that had made his request so ridiculous. He thanked his stars that he had held his tongue about the other thing. Ah, what a fool he had been! He could not have borne it, had the other been received with the same derision.

"I shall give you my prayer-book," she said at last, wiping her eyes and looking less amused than he had expected. "I've had it many years and value it dearly. It is prettily bound in Russia, and if you carry it on the proper place romance will see that it stops a bullet - though a Bible, I believe, is the more correct."

Somehow her tone sounded less cordial. She had withdrawn her hands, and her humour, at such a moment, jarred on him. In spite of his good resolutions he had managed to put his foot into it after all. Perhaps she had begun to suspect his secret and was displeased. He departed feeling utterly wretched and out of heart, and got very scant comfort from his book, for it only reminded him of how seriously he had compromised himself. He was in two minds whether or not to send it back, but decided not to do so in fear lest he might give fresh offence. The next day at dawn the Dixie sailed for the scene of war.

Lloyd Osbourne

III

Then followed the historic days of the blockade; the first landing on Cuba; the suspense and triumph attending Cervera's capture; El Caney; San Juan Hill; Santiago; and the end of the war. Howard Quintan fell ill with fever and was early invalided home; but Raymond stayed to the finish, an obscure spectator, often an obscure actor, in that world-drama of fleets and armies. Tried in the fire, his character underwent some noted changes. He developed unexpected aptitudes, became a marksman of big guns, showed resource and skill in boat-work, earned the repeated commendations of his superiors. He put his resolutions to the test, and emerged, surprised, thankful, and satisfied, to find that he was a brave man. He rose in his own esteem; it was borne in on him that he had qualities that others often lacked; it was inspiriting to win a reputation for daring, fearlessness, and responsibility.

He wrote when he could to his mother and Miss Latimer, and at rare intervals was sometimes fortunate enough to hear in turn from them. His mother was ill; the strain of his absence and danger was telling on her enfeebled constitution; she said she could not have got along at all had it not been for Miss Latimer's great kindness. It seemed that the old maid was her constant visitor, bringing her flowers, taking her drives, comforting her in the dark hours when her courage was nigh spent. "A good and noble woman," wrote the old lady, "and very much in love with my boy."

That line rang in Raymond's head long afterwards. He read it again and again, bewildered, tempted and yet afraid to believe it true, moved to the depths of his nature, at once happy and unhappy in the gamut of his doubts. It could not be possible. No, it could not be possible. Standing at the breech of his gun, his eyes on a Spanish gunboat they had driven under the shelter of a fort, he found himself repeating: "And very much in love with my boy. And very much in love with my boy." And then, suddenly becoming intent again on the matter in hand, he slammed the breech-mechanism shut and gave the enemy a six-inch shell.

Then there came the news of his mother's death. As much a victim of the war as any stricken soldier or sailor at the front, she was numbered on the roll of the fallen. The war had killed her as certainly, as surely, as any Mauser bullet sped from a tropic thicket. Raymond had only the consolation of knowing that Miss Latimer had been with her at the last and that she had followed his mother to the grave. Her letter, tender and pitiful, filled him with an inexpressible emotion. His little world now held but her.

This was the last letter he was destined to receive from her. The others, if there were others, all went astray in the chaotic confusion attendant on active service. The poor quartermaster, when the ship was so lucky as to take a mail aboard, grew accustomed to be told that there was nothing for him. He lost heart and stopped writing himself. What was the use, he asked himself? Had she not abandoned him? The critical days of the war were over; peace was assured; the victory won, the country was already growing forgetful of the victors. Such were his moody reflections as he paced the deck, hungry for the word that never came. Yes, he was forgotten. There could be no other explanation of that long silence. He was forgotten!

He returned in due course to New York and was paid off and mustered out of the service. It was dusk when he boarded an uptown car and stood holding to a strap, jostled and pushed about by the unheeding crowd. Already jealous of his uniform, he felt a little bitterness to see it regarded with such scant respect. He looked out of the windows at the lighted streets and wondered whether any of those hurrying thousands cared a jot for the men that had fought and died for them. The air, so sharp and chill after the tropics, served still further to dispirit him and add the concluding note of depression to his home-coming. He got off the car and walked down to Fifth Avenue, holding his breath as he drew near the Quintans' house. He rang the bell: waited and rang again. Then at last the door was unlocked and opened by an old woman.

"Is Miss - Mrs. Quintan at home?" he asked.

"Gone to Europe," said the old woman.

"But Miss Latimer?" he persisted.

"Gone to Europe," said the old woman.

"Mr. Howard Quintan?"

"Gone to Europe!"

He walked slowly down the steps, not even waiting to ask for their address abroad nor when they might be expected to return. They had faded into the immeasurable distance. What more was there to be said or hoped, and his dejected heart gave back the answer: nothing. He slept that night in a cheap hotel. The next day he bought a suit of civilian clothes and sought the office of the auditor's department. Here he received something more like a welcome. Many of the clerks, with whom he had scarcely been on nodding terms, now came up and shook him warmly by the hand. The superintendent sent for him and told him that his place had been held open, hinting, in the exuberance of the moment, at a slight increase of salary. The assistant superintendent made much of him and invited him out to lunch. The old darkey door-keeper greeted him like a long-lost parent. Raymond went back to his desk, and resumed with a sort of melancholy satisfaction the interrupted routine of twenty years. In a week he could hardly believe he had ever quitted his desk. He would shut his eyes and wonder whether the war had not been all a dream. He looked at his hands and asked himself whether they indeed had pulled the lanyards of cannon, lifted loaded projectiles, had held the spokes of the leaping wheel. His eyes, now intent on figures, had they in truth ever searched the manned decks of the enemy or trained the sights that had blown Spanish blockhouses to the four winds of heaven? Had it been he or his ghost who had stood behind the Nordenfeldt shields with the bullets pattering against the steel and stinging the air overhead? He or his ghost, barefoot in the sand that sopped the blood of fallen comrades, the ship shaking with the detonation of her guns, the hoarse cheering of her crew re-echoing in his half-deafened ears? A dream, yes; tragic and wonderful in the retrospect, filled with wild, bright pictures; incredible, yet true!

He was restless and lonely. He dreaded his evenings, which he knew not how to spend; dreaded the recurring Sunday, interminable in duration, whose leaden hours seemed never to reach their end. His only solace was in his work, which took him out of himself and prevented him from thinking. He made a weekly pilgrimage past the Quintans' house. The blinds were always drawn. It was as dead as one of those Cuban mills, standing in the desolation of burned fields. Once, greatly daring, and impelled by a sudden impulse, he went to the door and requested the address of his vanished friends:

"Grand Hotel, Vevey, Switzerland." He repeated the words to himself as he went back to his boarding-house, repeated them again and again like a child going on an errand, "Grand Hotel, Vevey, Switzerland," in a sort of panic lest he might forget them. He tossed that night in his bed in a torment of indecision. Ought he to write? Ought he to take the risk of a reply, courteous and cold, that he felt himself without the courage to endure? Or was it not better to put an end to it altogether and accept like a man the inevitable "no" of her decision.

He rose at dawn, and, lighting the gas, went back to bed with what paper he could lay his hands on. He had no pen, no ink, only the stub of a pencil he carried in his pocket. How it flew over the ragged sheets under the fierce spell of his determination! All the misery and longing of months went out in that letter. Inarticulate no longer, he found the expression of a passionate and despairing eloquence. He could not live without her; he loved her; he had always loved her; before he had been daunted by the inequality between them, but now he must speak or die. At the end he asked her, in set old-fashioned terms, whether or not she would marry him.

He mailed it as it was, in odd sheets and under the cover of an official envelope of the railroad company. He dropped it into the box and walked away, wondering whether he wasn't the biggest fool on earth and the most audacious, and yet stirred and trembling with a strange satisfaction. After all he was a man; he had lived as a man should, honorably and straightforwardly; he had the right to ask such a question of any woman and the right to an honest and considerate answer. Be it yes or no, he could reproach himself no longer with perhaps having let his happiness slip past him. The matter would be put beyond a doubt for ever, and if it went against him, as in the bottom of his heart he felt assured it would, he would try to bear it with what fortitude he might. She would know that he loved her. There was always that to comfort him. She would know that he loved her.

He got a postal guide and studied out the mails. He learned the names of the various steamers, the date of their sailing and arriving, the distance of Vevey from the sea. Were she to write on the same day she received his letter, he might hear from her by the Touraine. Were she to wait a day, her answer would be delayed for the Normandie. All this, if the schedule was followed to the letter and bad weather or accident did not intervene. The shipping page of the New York Herald became the only part of it he read. He scanned it daily with anxiety. Did it not tell him of his letter speeding over seas? For him no news was good news, telling him that all was well. He kept himself informed of the temperature of Paris, the temperature of Nice, and worried over the floods in Belgium. From the gloomy offices of the railroad he held all Europe under the closest scrutiny.

Then came the time when his letter was calculated to arrive. In his mind's eye he saw the Grand Hotel at Vevey, a Waldorf-Astoria set in snowy mountains with attendant Swiss yodelling on inaccessible summits, or getting marvels of melody out of little hand-bells, or making cuckoo clocks in top-swollen chalets. The letter would be brought to her on a silver salver, exciting perhaps the stately curiosity of Mrs. Quintan and questions embarrassing to answer. It was a pity he used that railroad envelope! Or would it lie beside her plate at breakfast, as clumsy and unrefined as himself, amid a heap of scented notes from members of the nobility? Ah, if he could but see her face and read his fate in her blue eyes!

When he returned home that night there was a singular-looking telegram awaiting him on the hall table. His hands shook as he took it up for it suddenly came over him that it was a cable. It had never occurred to him that she might do that; that there was anything more expeditious than the mail.

"Sailing by Touraine arriving sixth Christine Latimer."

He read and re-read it until the type grew blurred. What did it mean? He asked himself that a thousand times. What did it mean? He sought his room and locked the door, striding up and down with agitation, the cablegram clenched in his hand. He was beside himself, triumphant and yet in a fever of misgiving. Was it not perhaps a coincidence - not an answer to his own letter, but one of those extraordinary instances of what is called telepathy? Her words would bear either interpretation. Possibly the whole family was returning with her. Possibly she had never seen his letter at all. Possibly it was following her back to America, unopened and undelivered.

"Sailing by Touraine arriving sixth." Was that an

answer? Perhaps indeed it was. Perhaps it was a woman's way of saying "yes"; it might even be, in her surpassing kindness, that she was coming to break her refusal as gently as she might, too considerate of his feelings to write it baldly on paper. At least, amid all these doubts, it assured him of one thing, her regard; that he was not forgotten; that he had been mistaken in thinking himself ignored.

He spent the next eight days in a cruel and heart-breaking suspense. He could hardly eat or sleep. He grew thin and started at a sound. He paid a dollar to have the Touraine's arrival telegraphed to the office; another dollar to have it telegraphed to the boarding-house; he was fearful that one or the other might miscarry, and repeatedly warned the landlady of a possible message for him in the middle of the night.

"It means a great deal to me," he said. "It means everything to me. I don't know what I'd do if I missed the Touraine!"

Of course he did not miss the Touraine. He was on the wharf hours before her coming. He exasperated every-one with his questions. He was turned out of all kinds of barriers; he earned the distrust of the detectives; he became a marked man. He was certainly there for no good, that tall guy in the slouch hat, his lean hands fidgeting for a surreptitious pearl-necklace or an innocent-looking umbrella full of diamonds - one who, in their language, was a guy that would bear watching.

The steamer came alongside, and Raymond gazed up at the tier upon tier of faces. At length, with a catch in his heart, he caught sight of Miss Latimer, who smiled and waved her hand to him. He scanned her narrowly for an answer to his doubts; and these increased the more he gazed at her. It seemed a bad sign to see her so calm, so composed; worse still to see her occasionally in animated conversation with some of her fellow-passengers. He thought her smiles had even a perfunctory friendliness, and he had to share them besides with others. It was plain she had never received his letter. No woman could bear herself like that who had received such a letter. Then too she appeared so handsome, so high-bred, so charming and noticeable a figure in the little company about her that Raymond felt a peremptory sense of his own humbleness and of the impassable void between them. How had he ever dared aspire to this beautiful woman, and the thought of his effrontery took him by the throat.

He stood by the gangway as the passengers came off, an interminable throng, slow moving, teetering on the slats, a gush of funnelled humanity, hampered with bags, hat-boxes, rolls of rugs, dressing-cases, golf-sticks, and children. At last Miss Latimer was carried into the eddy, her maid behind her carrying her things, lost to view save by the bright feather in her travelling bonnet. The seconds were like hours as Raymond waited. He had a peep of her, smiling and patient, talking over her shoulder to a big Englishman behind her. Then, as the slow stream brought her down, she stepped lightly on the wharf, turned to Raymond, and, before he could so much as stammer out a word, flung her arms round his neck and kissed him.

"Did you really want me?" she said; and then, "You gave me but two hours to catch the old Touraine!"

THE MASCOT OF BATTERY B

Battery A had a mascot goat, and Battery C a Filipino kid, and Battery D a parrot that could swear in five languages, but I guess we were the only battery in the brigade that carried an old lady! Filipino, nothing! But white as yourself and from Oakland, California, and I don't suppose I'd be here talking to you now, if it hadn't been for her.

I had known Benny a long time - Benny was her son, you know, the only one she had - and when I enlisted at the beginning of the war Benny wished to do it, too, only he was scared to death, not of the Spaniards, but his old Ma! So he hung off and on, while I drilled at the Presidio and rode free on the street cars, and did the little hero act, and ate pie the whole day long. My! How they used to bring us pies in them times and boxes of see-gars - and flowers! Flowers to burn! Well I remember a Wisconsin regiment marching along Market Street, big splendid men from the up-North woods, every one of them with a Calla lily stuck in his gun! Oh, it was fine, with the troops pouring in, and the whole city afire to receive them, and the girls almost cutting the clothes off your back for souvenirs - and it made Benny sick to see it all, him clerking in a hardware store and eating his heart out to go with the boys. He hung back as long as he could, but at last he couldn't stand it no longer, and the day before we sailed he went and enlisted in my battery.

He knew there was going to be a rumpus at home and I suppose that was why he put it off to the very end, not wanting to be plagued to death or cried over. But when he got into his uniform and had done a spell of goose-step with the first sergeant, he was so blamed rattled about going home that he had to take me along too. He lived away off somewheres in a poorish sort of neighbourhood, all little frame houses and little front yards about that big, where you could see commuters watering Calla lilies in their city clothes. Benny's house seemed the smallest and poorest of the lot, though it had Calla lilies too and other sorts of flowers, and a mat with "welcome" on it, and some kind of a dog that licked our hands as we walked up the front steps and answered to the name of Dook.

Benny pushed open the door and went in, me at his heels, and both of us nervous as cats. His mother was sitting in a rocker, reading the evening paper with gold spectacles, and I never saw such a straight-backed old lady in my life, nor any so tall and thin and commanding. She looked up at us, kind of startled to see two soldiers walking into her kitchen, and Benny smiled a silly smile and said:

"Mommer, I'm off to help Dooey in the Fillypines!"

I guess he thought she'd jump at him or something, for he had always been a mother's boy and minded everything she said, though he was twenty-eight years old and rising-nine - but all she did was to draw in her breath sharp and sudden, so you could hear the whistle of it, and then two big tears rolled out under her specs.

"Don't feel bad about it, Mommer," said Benny in a snuffly voice.

She never said a word, but got up from the chair and came over to where Benny was, very white and trembly, and looking at his army coat like it was a shroud.

"Oh, my son, my son!" she said, kind of choking over the words.

"I couldn't stay behind when all the boys was going," he said.

I saw he was holding back all he could to keep from crying, and I didn't blame him either, as we was to sail the next day and the old lady was his Ma. It's them good-byes that break a soldier all up. So I lit out and played with the dog and made him jump through my hands and fetch sticks and give his paw (he was quite a RE-markable dog, that dog, though his breeding wasn't much), while I could hear them inside, talking and talking, and the old lady's voice running on about the danger of drink and how he mustn't sleep in wet clothes or give back-talk to his officers - it was wonderful the horse-sense that old lady had - and how he must respeck the uniform he wore and be cheerful and willing and brave, like his sainted father who was dead - all that mothers say and sometimes what soldiers do - and through it all there was a pleasant rattle of dishes and the sound of the fire being poked up, and Benny asking where's the table-cloth, and was there another pie? By and by I was called in, and there, sure enough, the table was spread, and we were both made to sit down while the old lady skirmished around and wiped her eyes when we weren't looking.

We had beefsteak, warmed-over pigs' feet, coffee, potato cakes, fresh lettuce, Graham gems, and two kinds of pie, and the next day we sailed for Manila.

Them early days in the Fillypines was the toughest proposition I was ever up against. Things hadn't settled down as they did afterward, nobody knowing where he was at, and all of us shoved up to the front higgeldy-piggeldy; and, being Regulars, they gave us the heavy end of it, having to do all the fighting while the Volunteers was being taught the difference between a Krag-Jorgensen and a Moro Castle. It was all front in them days - for the Regulars! But we were lucky in our commissary sergeant, a splendid young man named Orr, and we lived well from the start and never came down to rations. The battery got quite a name for having griddle-cakes for breakfast and carrying a lot of dog generally in the eating line, and someone wrote a song, to the toon of Chickamauga, called "The Fried Chicken of Battery B." But I tell you, it wasn't all fried chicken either, for the fighting was heavy and hot, and a good many of the boys pegged out. If ever there was a battery that looked for trouble and got it - it was Battery B! But we took good care of our commissary sergeant - did I mention he was a splendid young man named Orr? - and though we dropped a good many numbers, wounded, dead, sick, and missing - we kep' up the good name of the battery and had canned butter and pop-overs nearly every day.

Benny and I were chums, but nobody knows what that word means till you've kept warm under the same blanket and kneeled side by side in the firing-line. It brings men together like nothing else in the world, and it's queer the unlikely sorts that take to one another. I was so common and uneddicated that I wonder what

Benny ever saw to like in me, for, as I said, he was a regular Mommer's boy and splendidly brought up and an electrician. Religious, too, and a church member! But he was powerful fond of me, and never went into action but what he'd let off a little prayer to himself that I might come out all right and go to heaven if bolo-ed. Pity he hadn't taken as much trouble for himself, for one day while we were lying in a trench, and firing for all we were worth, I suddenly saw that look in his face that a soldier gets to know so well.

"Benny, you're shot!" I yelled out, dropping my Krag and all struck of a heap.

"Shot, nothing!" he answered, and then he keeled over in the dirt and his legs began to kick.

He took a powerful long time to die, and there was even some talk of sending him down to the base hospital, the field one being that full and constantly needed at our heels. But he pleaded with the doctors and was allowed as a favour to stay on and die where he was minded - with the battery. I was with him all I could, and I'll never forget how good that commissary sergeant was, a splendid young man named Orr, who always had a little pot of chicken broth for Benny and cornstarch, and what he fancied most of all - a sort of thick dough cakes we called sinkers. As luck would have it I got into trouble about this time - a little matter of two silver candle-sticks and a Virgin's crown - and Benny sent for Captain Howard (it was him that commanded the battery), and weak as he was, dying, he begged me off, and the captain swore awful to hide how bad he felt, and struck my name off the sheet to please him. There was little enough to do in this line, for it was plain as day where Benny was bound for, and he knew himself he would never see that little home in Oakland again.

Well, he got worse and worse, and sometimes when I went there he didn't know me, being out of his head or kind of dopy with the doctor's stuff, the shadow being over him, as Irish people say. One night he was that low that I got scared, and I waylaid the contract surgeon as he came out.

"Doctor," I said, "it's all up with Benny, ain't it?"

"He'll never hear reveille no more," he says.

I got my blanket and lay outside the door, it being against regulations for any of us to be in the field-hospital after taps. But the orderly said he'd call me if Benny was to wake up before the end, and the doctor promised me I might go in. Sure enough, I was called somewheres along of four o'clock and the orderly led me inside the tent to Benny's cot. There was no light but a candle in a bottle, and I held it in my hand and bent over and looked in Benny's face. He was himself all right, and he put his cold, sweaty hand in mine and pressed it.

"Do you know me, old man?" I said. "Do you know me?"

"Good-bye, Bill," he said, and then, as I leaned over him, his voice being that low and faint - he whispered: "Billy, I guess you'll have to rustle for another chum!"

Them was his last words and he said them with a kind of a smile, like he was happy and didn't give a damn to live. Then the little life he had left went out. The orderly looked at his watch, and then wrote the time on a slate after Benny's regimental number and the word: "died." This was about all the epitaph he got, though we buried him properly in the morning and gave him the usual send-off. Then his effects was auctioned off in front of the captain's tent, a nickel for this, ten cents for that - a soldier hasn't much at any time, you know, and on the march less than a little - and five-sixty about covered the lot. There was quite a rush for the picture of his best girl, but I bought it in, along with one of his Ma and a one-pound Hotchkiss shell and the hilt of a Spanish officer's sword; and when I had laid them away in my haversack and had borrowed a sheet of paper and an envelope from the commissary sergeant to write to Benny's mother, it came over me what a little place a man fills in the world and how things go on much the same without him.

I was setting down to write that letter and was about midway through, having got to "the pride of the battery and regretted by all who noo him," when I looked up, and what in thunder do you suppose I saw? The old lady herself, by God! walking into camp with an umberella and a valise, and looking like she always did - powerful grim and commanding. Someone must have told her the news and which was my tent, for she walked straight up to where I was and said: "William, William!" like that. She didn't cry or nothing, and anybody at a distance might have thought she was just talking to a stranger; but there was a whole funeral march in the sound of her voice, and you could read Benny's death like print in her wrinkled old face. I took her out to where we had buried him, and she plumped down on her knees and prayed, with the umberella and the valise beside her, while I held my hat in one hand and my pistol in the other, ready for any bolo business that might come out of the high grass.

Then we went back to the field-hospital and had a look in, she explaining on the way how she had mortgaged her home, so as to come and look after Benny. I guess the hospital must have appeared kind of cheerless, for lots of the wounded were lying on the bare ground, and it was a caution the way some of them groaned and groaned. You see Battery K had just come in, having had an engagement by the way at Dagupan, and Wilson's cavalry, besides, had dumped a sight of their men on us.

"And it was in a place like this that my boy died?" said the old lady, her mouth quivering and then closing on the words like a steel trap.

"There's the very cot, Ma'am," I said.

She said something like "Oh, oh, oh!" under her breath, and, taking out her handkerchief, wiped the face and lips of the man in the cot, who was lying there with his uniform still on him. I suppose he had got it because he was a bad case, - the cot, I mean, - and certainly he was far from spry.

"He's dead!" said the old lady, shuddering. "He's dead!"

"Orderly," I said, "number fifty-six is dead!"

The orderly bent over to make sure and then ran for his slate - the same old slate - and began to write down the same old thing. I suppose there was some sense to that slate racket, for with a little spit one slate would do for a brigade, but it seemed a cheap way to die. Then, as we stood there, another orderly came gallumphing in with something steaming in a tin can. The old lady took it out of his hand and smelled it, supercilious.

"What do you call this?" she said.

"It's chicken broth, Ma'am," he said. "That's what it is, Ma'am."

"Faugh!" said the old lady, "faugh!" and handed it back to him, like she was going to throw it away, but didn't. Then we watched him dip it out in tin cups and carry it around, while some other fellers came in and carried out the body of the man in the cot, a trooper by his legs. We went out with them, and, I tell you, it was good to stand in the open air again and breathe. The old lady took a little spell of rest on a packing-case; then she gave me her umberella and valise to take back to quarters, and, rolling up her sleeves, made like she was going into the hospital again.

I didn't know what to say, but I guess I looked it.

"William," she said, with a glitter of her gold specs.

"Ma'am," said I.

"Those boys aren't getting proper CON-sideration," she said. "If it was dogs," she said, "they couldn't be treated worse. William, I'm going to see what one old woman can do."

"You ought to ask Captain Howard first," I said. "You don't belong to the Army Medical Corps."

"It's them that let Benny die," she said, with her eyes

snapping, "and, as for asking, they'd say 'No,' for they don't allow any women except at the base hospitals."

I knew this for a fack, but I'd rather she'd find it out from the captain than from me. I didn't want to seem to make trouble for her. So, while I was wondering what to do about it, she headed right in, leaving me with the valise and the umberella, and a kind of qualmy feeling that the old lady might strike a snag.

I didn't have no chance to come back till along sundown, but, my stars I even in that time there had been a change. Benny's mother had been getting in her deadly work, and the orderlies were bursting mad, not that any of them dared say anything outright or show it except in their faces, which were that long; for, you see, the contract surgeon had taken her side, and had backed her up. But they moved around like mules with their ears down, powerful unwilling, and yet scared to say a word. The hospital had been made a new place, with another tent up that had been laid away and forgotten (you wouldn't think it possible, but it was), and the sick and wounded had been sorted over and washed and made comfortable; and, where before there was no room to turn around, you could walk through wide lanes and wonder what had become of the crowd. She had peeked into the cooking, too, and had found out more things going wrong in five hours than the contract surgeon had in five months. Blest if there wasn't a court-martial laying for every one of the orderlies if they said "boo!" for the swine had been making away scandalous with butter and chocolate and beef - tea and canned table peaches and sparrow-grass and sardines, and all the like of that, belly-robbing the boys right and left perfectly awful.

It was a mighty good account of the contract surgeon that he took it all so well, and was willing to admit how badly he had been done. But he was a splendid young fellow, named Marcus, and what the old lady said, went! He was right sorry he couldn't put her on the strength of the battery, but the regulations kept women nurses at the base-hospitals, and anyway (for we broke everything them days, and there wasn't enough red-tape left to play cat-and-my-cradle with) Captain Howard hated the sight of a petticoat, and was dead set against women anywheres. I don't know what they had ever done to him, but I'm just saying it for a fack. But, however it was, Marcus said the old lady had to be kept out of sight, or else the captain would surely send her to the rear under arrest.

Now, this made it a pretty hard game for the old lady to play, and you can reckon how much dodging she had to do to keep out of the captain's sight. It was hard about her sleeping, too, for she had to do that where she could, not to speak of the pay she might have drawn and didn't, and which, sakes alive! she earned twenty times over. By and by everybody got onto it except the captain, but there wasn't such a skunk in the battery as to tell him, partly because of the joke, but, most of all, on account of the convalescents, who naturally thought a heap of her. Then it got whispered around that she was our mascot, and carried the luck of the battery; and it was certainly RE-markable how it began to change, getting fresh beef quite regular and maple syrup to burn, and nine kegs of Navy pickles by mistake.

You would have thought she was too old to stand it, for we was always on the move, and I have seen her sleeping on what was nothing else but mud, with the rain coming down tremenjous. But she was a tough old customer, and always came to time, outlasting men that could have tossed her in the air, or run with her a block and never taken breath. But, of course, it couldn't be kept up for ever - I mean about the captain - and, sure enough, one day he caught her riding on a gun-carriage, while he was passing along the line on a Filipino pony.

"Good God!" he said, like that, reining in his horse and looking at her campaign hat and the old gingham dress she wore. I wonder she didn't correct him for his profanity, but I allow for once she was scared stiff, and hadn't no answer ready. My! But she kind of shrunk in and looked a million years old.

"Madam," said he, "do you belong to this column?"

"Unofficially, I do," she said, perking up a little.

"Might I inquire where you came from?" said he, doing the ironical perlite.

"Oakland, California," said she.

"And is this your usual mode of locomotion?" said he. "Riding on a gun?" said he. "Like the Goddess of War," said he. "Perching on the belcherous cannon's back," said he.

The old lady, now as bold as brass, allowed that it was.

"Scandalous!" roared the captain. "Scandalous!"

The old lady always had a kind of nattified air, and even on a gun-carriage she sported that look of dropping in on the neighbours for a visit. She ran up her little parasol, settled her feet, give a tilt to her specs, and looked the captain in the eye.

"Yes," she said, "I do belong to this column, and I guess it would be a smaller column by a dozen, if it hadn't been for me in your field-hospital. Or twenty," said she. "Or maybe more," said she.

This kind of staggered the captain. It was plain he didn't know just what to do. We were hundreds of miles from anywheres, and there were Aguinaldoes all around us. He was as good as married to that old lady, for any means he had of getting rid of her. He began to look quite old himself, as he stared and stared at the mascot of Battery B, the cannon lumping along, and the old lady bouncing up and down, as the wheels sank to the axles in the rutty road.

"When we strike the railroad, home you go," said he.

"We'll see about that," said the old lady.

"It's disgraceful," said he. "Pigging with a whole battery," said he. "Oh, the shame of it!" said he.

"Shoulder-straps don't always make a gentleman," said she.

"Holy Smoke!" said he, galloping off very fierce and grand on his little horse, to haul Dr. Marcus over the coals. They say the contract surgeon got it in the neck, but we were short-handed in that department already, Dr. Fenelly having been killed in action, so the captain could do nothing worse nor reprimand him. It was bad enough as it was - for Marcus - for HE wasn't no old lady, and the captain could let himself rip. And, I tell you, it was a caution any time to be up against Captain Howard, for, though he could be nice as pie and perlite to beat the band, it only needed the occasion for him to unloose on you like a thirteen-inch gun.

Well, it was perfectly lovely what happened next, for, with all her sassiness, the old lady felt pretty blue, and talked about Benny for hours, like she always did when she was down-hearted; and, by this time, you know, she had got to love Battery B, and every boy in it; and it naturally went against her to think of starting out all over again with strangers, and them maybe Volunteers. So you can guess what her feelings was that night when the captain went down with fever. It was like getting money from home!

The captain had never been sick in his life, and he took it hard to be laid by and keep off the flies, while another feller ran the battery and jumped his place. I guess it came over him that he wasn't the main guy after all, and that it wouldn't matter a hill of beans whether he lived or quit. Them's one of the things you learn in hospital, and the most are the better for it; but the captain, you see, was getting his lesson a bit late. So he was layed off, with amigos to carry him or bolo him (like what amigos are when they get a chance), and the old lady give a whoop and took him in charge. My! If she wasn't good to that man. and, as for coals of fire, she regularly slung them at him! The doctor, too, got his little axe in, and was everlastingly praising the old lady, and telling the captain he would have been a goner, if it hadn't been for her! And, when the captain grew better - which he did after a few days - he was that meek he'd eat out of your hand. The old lady was not only a champion nurse, but she was a buster to cook. Give her a ham-bone and a box of matches and she could turn out a French dinner of five courses, with oofs-sur-le-plate, and veal-cutlets in paper pants! It was then, I reckon, she settled the captain for good; and, when he picked up and was able to walk about camp, leaning pretty heavy on her arm, she called him "George" and "My boy" - like that - and you might have taken him for Benny and she his Ma.

There was nothing too good for the old lady after that, and the captain wouldn't hear of her living anywheres but at the officers' mess, where she sat at his right hand, and always spoke first. The Queen of England couldn't have been treated with more respeck, and the captain put her on the strength of the battery, and she drew back-pay from the day she first blew into camp. My, but it was changed times! and you ought to have seen the way the old lady cocked her head in the air and made a splendid black silk dress of loot, which she wore every evening with the officers and rattled all over with jet. But it didn't turn her head the least bit, like for a time the boys feared it might, and she was twice as good to us as she had been before. We had a pull at headquarters now, and she had a heart that big that it could hold the officers and us, too - and more in the draw.

The tide had turned her way when she needed it most, for, tough as she was, she could not have long gone on like she had been. She had worn down very thin, and was like a shadow of the old lady I remembered in Oakland, California, and kind of sunk in around the eyes, and I don't believe Benny would have known her, had he risen from the grave; and, when anybody joked with her about it, and said: "Take it easy, Ma'am, you owe it to the battery to be keerful," she'd answer she

Lloyd Osbourne

had enlisted for the term of the war, and looked to peg out the day peace was proclaimed.

"Then I'll be off to join Benny," she'd say, "and the rest of the battery, in heaven!"

There was getting to be a good deal of a crowd up there - that is, if the other place hadn't yanked them in - and some of the boys found a lot of comfort in her way of thinking.

"A boy as dies for his country isn't going to be bothered about passing in," she would say, with a click of her teeth and that sure way of hers like she KNEW. And I, reckon perhaps she DID.

One afternoon she was suddenly taken very bad; and, instead of better, she grew worse and worse, being tied to the bed and raving; and the captain, who wouldn't hear of her being sent to hospital, give up his own quarters to her and almost went crazy, he was that frightened she was dying.

"It's just grit that's kep' her alive," I heard the doctor saying to him.

"You must save her, Marcus," said the captain, holding to him, like he was pleading with the doctor for her life. "You must save her, Marcus. You must do everything in the world you can, Marcus."

The contract surgeon looked mighty glum. "She's like a ship that's been burning up her fittings for lack of coal," said he. "There ain't nothing left," he said. "Not a damn thing," said he, and then he piled in a lot of medical words that seemed to settle the matter.

As for the captain, he sat down and regularly cried. I'm sorry now I said anything against the captain, for he was a splendid man, and the pride of the battery. And, I tell you, he wasn't the only one that cried neither, for the boys idolised the old lady, and there wasn't no singing that night or cards or anything. I was on picket, and it was a heavy heart I took with me into the dark; and, when they left me laying in the grass, and nobody nearer nor a hundred yards and that behind me, I felt mortal blue and lonesome and homesick, and like I didn't care whether I was killed or not. It was midnight when I went out, - mind, I say MIDNIGHT - and I don't know what ailed me that night, for, after thinking of the old lady and Benny and my own mother that was dead, and all the rest of the boys that had marched out so fine and ended so miserable - I couldn't keep the sleep away; and I'd go off and off, though I tried my damnedest not to; and my eyes would shut in spite of me and just glue together; and I would kind of drown, drown, drown in sleep. If ever a man knew what he was doing, and the risk, and what I owed to the boys, and me a Regular, and all that - it was ME; yet - yet - And you must remember it had been a hard day, and the guns had stuck again and again in the mud, and it was pull, mule, pull, soldier, till you thought you'd drop in your tracks. Oh, I am not excusing myself! I've seen men shot for sleeping on guard, and I know it's right; and, even in my dreams, I seemed to be reproaching myself and calling myself a stinker.

Then, just as I was no better nor a log, laying there with my head on my arm, a coward and a traitor, and a black disgrace to the uniform I wore, I suddenly waked up with somebody shaking me hard, real rough, like that - and I jumped perfectly terrible to think it might be the captain on his rounds. Oh, the relief when I saw it was nothing else than the old lady, she kneeling beside me all alone, and her specs shining in the starlight.

"William, William!" she said, sorrowful and warning, her voice kind of strange, like she didn't want to say out loud that I had been asleep at my post; and, as she drew away her hand, it touched mine, and it was ice-cold. And, just as I was going to tell her to lope back and be keerful of herself, the grass rustled in front of me, and I saw, rising like a wall, rows on rows of Filipino heads! My, but didn't I shoot and didn't I run, and the bugles rang out and the whole line was rushed, me pelting in and the column spitting fire along a length of three miles! We stood them off all right, and my name was mentioned in orders, and I was promoted sergeant, the brigadier shaking my hand and telling the boys I was a pattern to go by and everything a Regular ought to be. But it wasn't THAT I was going to tell. It was about the old lady, though I didn't learn it till the next day.

She had died at a quarter of midnight, and had lain all night on the captain's bed with a towel over her poor old face.

Now, what do you make of that?

www.ingramcontent.com/pod-product-compliance
Lightning Source LLC
Chambersburg PA
CBHW051827170626
46807CB00003B/1059